Teenage Bluez III

A collection of urban stories

Life Changing Books in conjunction with Power Play Media
Published by Life Changing Books
P.O. Box 423 Brandywine, MD 20613

Library of Congress Cataloging-in-Publication Data;

www.lifechangingbooks.net

ISBN- (10)1-934230979 (13) 978-1934230978
Copyright ® 2009

Acknowledgements

The authors of Teenage Bluez III would like to thank God for guiding our hands and thoughts to write these stories. Prayerfully these stories will help teenagers from all over the world who have or are experiencing similar situations. We would also like to thank our parents, who gave us unconditional support along with our friends. To Kevin Carr, thanks for designing another great cover. Also, a big thanks goes to all the bookstores, and the distributors who push any of the Teenage Bluez series. Your support is truly appreciated. Lastly, to Life Changing Books, we thank you for giving us an amazing opportunity.

TEENAGE BLUEZ SERIES 3

Table of Contents

MYSPACE CRAZE

by Khadijah Knight

I sat in a funk with my legs spread apart and my arms folded as my teacher spoke loudly.

"Okay guys, remember to review unit sixteen and prepare yourselves for the unit test next week. Have a great day," Mrs. Moses announced.

"So, when is the test again? Monday?" a student yelled out.

"You can come to school on Monday if you would like but no one is going to be here. It's our teacher's administrative day. The test is on Tuesday when you return sweetheart," she reminded him.

OMG! I'd totally forgotten, and I'm sure everyone else did too judging by the way we all cheered in unison like middle school students. Prince Georges County was known to give out more half-days and breaks than any other county in Maryland. But I'm not complaining. I was so grateful for getting out early for half-a-day and having Monday off too. I needed the three day break from Lake Clifton High. I quickly gathered my things and proceeded to exit the classroom.

I hated traveling the crowded hallways, I thought to myself as I headed to meet my girl, Lauren. I was considered an introvert to most. I simply stuck with my small crew and allowed no extra chicken-heads to enter my small circle. That fact was proven as I walked down the hall without even looking at anyone, and certainly not cracking a smile.

Even though our school was set up as co-ed, they got

1

us split like we're in some sort of penitentiary or something. The school is large enough that all the boys are on the lower level and all the girls are on the upper level. The administrators definitely don't play. They don't care if your mama got lost on the wrong floor and you tried to find her, your butt will be in for it.

"Anondi!" Lauren screamed to me from down the hall. I turned around to meet her halfway.

"Hey, L you ready to go?" I asked.

"Yup, let me just get one thing from the locker."

On the way over to her locker I was reminded of Lauren's popularity. She was dressed in her Juicy Couture sweat suit and that's only, because it was Friday. Any other day you'd think it was a fashion show. She was known to wear fancy belts, scarves, and high-dollar accessories.

Somehow within minutes, people from everywhere swarmed us spitting compliments like they'd gotten paid to do so. The majority of all the females either spoke to Lauren to get close, or they threw mug shots to show how much they envied her. There were girls walking up to her complimenting her on her outfit, and her perfect hair.

Lauren was definitely confident enough to intimidate you. I wondered how that happened since we were both underclassman. She even had the seniors kissing butt. I watched Lauren as she gave each of her admirers some play. She was full of life in every way, even down to the way she laughed and showed off her overbite.

It just makes me laugh, because to me she's the same petite, dark-skinned girl I met back in elementary school. The only difference is she had a edgy short cut resembling Rhianna's and she had the body to match.

Unlike me, I continued to rock the natural look. My hair stays either blow dried straight or curly from being wet. My frame remained small too, but slender and toned from years of in-

2

tense ballet training.

But one thing was for sure, Lauren wasn't Rhianna, and I wasn't a part of her entourage so she needed to hurry it up. I was ready to leave the school grounds, and start my three day weekend.

"L, let's go," I snapped.

"Okay girl, I'm ready. I had to make sure my lip gloss was poppin'," she said as she took one last pucker in the mirror of her locker.

"I bet. Now let's roll," I smirked.

When we entered the school parking lot it seemed as if we had just walked into a party. All of the students had their music blasting from their cars, and most of the dudes were all posted up somewhere watching the honeys go by. Lauren fit right in with the wild crowd, but I was definitely not the type to lollygag.

I started walking faster allowing the crisp, spring breeze to whip through my hair. I really wanted to stick to my afternoon routine. I'd show up at school, do my work, and leave. Unlike Lauren, the social butterfly, she knew everybody, so as suspected, she wanted to go mingle with some of the other people sitting on top of the picnic tables on the side of the building.

"Nondi, I'll be right back. I have to holler at Kevin real quick," she said not even giving me the opportunity to protest. She just walked off, but I had something for that.

"Two minutes!" I yelled to her.

On my way over to my car, I could feel my daily migraine coming on. I never understood what it could be. My dad said it was probably stress, which was possible, but I didn't think so. Sometimes it got so bad, to the point where I couldn't even keep my eyes open. My dad had taken me to see a doctor but all they said was that they couldn't find anything. They did give me some Percocet to ease the pain. I normally took them at night, or when I wasn't doing anything that required me to be alert. The pills definitely do the job, because I'd been out cold on many different occasions. I just prayed that it wouldn't get too bad while driving home. I sat on the hood of my 2003 Honda accord trying to relax, when I noticed a text had come through on my sidekick. I got excited. I loved my phone and sent text messages day in and day out.

Wats up wit u.
u looked beautiful today.

I typed back…real quick. I didn't think I looked so great today but if I had an admirer I wanted to know who he was.

Who is this?
I don't recognize the number.

I waited… and waited, but didn't get a response. The person probably realized they had the wrong number.

From the looks of it, Lauren didn't want a ride home. She was still consumed by Kevin, her loser boyfriend. I believe I did say two minutes, I reminded myself just as my phone rang.

"Yes, chick." I always called Lauren that when I got pissed. "What's up?"

"I'm going to come to your house around five. I'm gonna go chill with Kevin for now. Is that cool?"

"Sure L. Don't do anything I wouldn't do. BYE!"

"Girl it's not even like that," she assured me, then waved crazily with an animated smile. "See ya later."

I rolled my eyes, because she was so predictable. I hopped in my car and started on my way to Simmons Estates better known as home. Since I lived in Accokeek Maryland, it wasn't too far away from school. The area was known to be nice and peaceful, but when I adjusted my mirror something caught my eye. I saw a black Crown Vic parked near the front gate of the community, but facing my car. It had tinted windows and the driver's seat window was rolled down a little. I couldn't make out the person inside but it sure seemed a little suspicious. When I looked back for a closer look, whoever it was drove off. That was weird but whatever, I told myself.

═══════════════

When I walked inside my front door, MeMe greeted me in the foyer. She jumped on me giving mommy kisses as members of my family always did. Me-Me, an all white Pomeranian, loved me to death, and I loved her right back just like she was blood. She was a gift from my mom when I turned eleven. We named her MeMe, because she thinks everything is all about her. She should, she's the baby around the Wade house-hold.

I put her down to go in to the office to say hello to my dad. It was always nice to see him working from home. He worked very long hours at the firm.

Attorney Jonathan Wade, was the name and getting celebrities out of jail was his game. He'd owned his own firm for years, but after my mom passed he's had to work extra hard to maintain a good lifestyle for my sister and I. I believe he'd done an awesome job, because we lived rather comfortably. It's just me, him, my sister Gabrielle, who's away in college and the dog.

When I rushed into the office, Dad was on the phone as usual. I picked the dog up who was right on my heels and sat her on my lap. I sat down to wait on him to end his call. When he saw me, he assured me in a whisper that he'd only need one more minute. Literally, a minute had passed and he was done.

"So, how's my baby girl?" he asked, while coming from around his desk to give me a kiss on the cheek.

"Good Daddy. Just got over a small headache, but I'm good so far."

"Wow, Anondi, you're still having those? Let's go back and see a doctor again."

"No, that's not necessary. It's probably nothing. It's just bothering me today."

"Is that why you're home so early?"

"No, we had a half day today. We don't go back until Tuesday."

"Oh, that's cool. Maybe we can hook up and do lunch this weekend and do some catching up. What do you say?" he asked.

I examined my Dad momentarily. He was so handsome and always dressed as if he were on his way to a board meeting. "Okay cool, Dad. Gabby is supposed to be coming home this weekend for spring break so that'll be perfect," I responded.

We both agreed. After that there was a small pause. It gave me a second to actually look my dad in the face. He seemed extra distinguished all of a sudden. He was tall, slim, and had a close hair cut, showing off his sporadic gray strands. He was a man of very high esteem, big on family pride, and wanted his children to be the same. He looked very tired though. I noticed the bags under his Asian-looking eyes that looked just like mine.

"Dad you look tired, why don't you go get some rest?" I said, rubbing his arm.

"I know baby girl but I've been working on this big case lately. That's been taking up all of my time. I got to get this thing squared away before I can get any rest."

"I know but at least an hour Dad. If you don't rest, your immune system will crash. This is not going anywhere I promise you," I assured him pointing around at the office.

"I know sweetheart. I promise you when I get this done

I'm going to get all the rest I need," he said.

"Okay Daddy, thank you." I hugged him one last time, and headed up to my room.

I hated the fact that my dad worked so hard. It was impossible for him to spend any time with family let alone rest. But like he says if he doesn't work, I don't eat. So I just take what he says and make sure that everything else is taken care of around the house. It's a five bedroom brick house with three floors. It's a traditional family home that's cozy yet elegant. Even though, it's a decent sized house, it's not hard to clean. We hardly go in any of the rooms, because no one is ever home. There are some rooms that are forbidden as well, because of expensive furniture or valuables. As long as the bathrooms, the dog's area, and the kitchen is clean on a daily basis, everything else works out fine.

I walked into my room and smiled. It was exactly the way I'd left. That was a surprise, because MeMe always got into everything. I jumped on the bed, stomach first to check my home phone messages. I had one new message from Gabrielle. I was always excited to hear from Gabby.

"Hey Nondi, it's me Gabby! I'm calling to tell you that I'll be there tomorrow around five in the evening. I definitely can't wait to see you. I have something to tell you when I get there. But anyway, got to get back to work! Love you. See you soon."

Wow, I wondered what the news was all about. I prayed she wasn't gonna come back to tell me she was moving to New York for good. I'd literally kill her. It was hard enough not having her in Maryland already. I simply adored my sister. We looked exactly alike, even though she had four years up on me. It was crazy, because we acted like twins…nobody could take her place. I owed her a lot. When my mom died I was only eleven years old, and she was just fifteen. She gave up a lot of things to make life easier on me and my dad. While she was still trying to finish high school, and then press her way to college, she still gave me help with homework, cooked the meals, and tried to get me to adjust to our new life without our mom. I give her thumbs up, because most people who've been through as much as we have would've cracked by now.

Luckily, Gabby had done well for her self. She was in her third year at NYU. Now, the pressure was all on me. I felt like I held down the fort pretty well. Most days I handled my chores, my schoolwork, and my entertainment; dancing and Myspace surfing.

The thought of Myspace hit me like an addict as I hopped into bed. I laid there looking around trying to think of something else to do besides getting on the computer. It seemed to be an addiction, and I'd been trying to wean myself into doing other things. I didn't have many friends other than Lauren and Corey, so when they weren't around life was super boring.

It was only 2:30 p.m. when I glanced over at the clock. Lauren told me that she would get to the house about five. Who knows what she was doing. Lately she'd been sticking under Kevin, and for what I didn't know. He was a loser type dude, reminded me of a guy that had sent me a friend request on Myspace.

That was it! I couldn't take it any longer. I hopped up to grab my laptop then plunged back onto the bed. I had to check my myspace page. When I logged in, I had an inbox full of messages already, and it was just mid-day. There was one guy in particular that I looked forward to hearing from on occasions. It's my buddy, Davon who seemed to be online more than I was. He wrote cool things to me and kept my interest. Not to mention the fact that he was kinda cute; except the gruesome looking tattoo that could be seen near the upper part of his neck. Hopefully, since I was looking at a photo, it didn't look that bad in person. He said he lived in the D.C. area and wanted to hook up. But when he wrote that he was twenty years old, I knew there was no chance we'd ever meet. Davon was just a nice person to talk to when I got bored, or stayed online in the wee hours of the night.

I tried to keep it simple with Davon so that I wouldn't lead him on. I had over five hundred Myspace friends, but spent more time talking to him than anyone. He even asked where I lived, which I thought was crazy. I told him he was getting too personal, and to keep it on a friendly note. I didn't even consider it. Internet dating was real tacky, and I was starting to get sleepy after twenty minutes of sending comments and posting bulletins.

I was done with Myspace for the day, and figured I'd get a nice little nap until Lauren arrived. I knew I wouldn't get any rest with her around. She was a compulsive night owl, and liked me to stay up with her so we could spend the whole night joking and talking. Just as I tried to get comfortable my phone rang. I knew exactly who it was going to be. It's about that time.

"Hi lil' boy…"

"Lil boy? I'm a grown man named, Corey the last time I checked," he said using a deep voice, making me laugh.

"Corey please, you are so silly. Yes, you might be eighteen but I'm sixteen, and I'll be grown before you. Technically at eighteen girls are grown and you sir can't say that until you are twenty-one. So I'm going to need for you…."

He cut me off.

"Alright that's enough. You proved your point. So what are you doing boo?"

"Boo?" Stop calling me that," I said, headed to lie on my furry carpet.

"You are my boo even if I'm not yours," Corey told

me. "So, just answer the question without arguments," he commanded. As he continued to talk, I started thinking back on how my relationship with Corey had changed over the years.

You see Corey and I had been friends for over ten years. His parents knew me and my dad loved Corey. When Corey first moved to our neighborhood my mother used to take me to play with him a lot. As long as I've known him he's had this crush on me and no matter what I did, I couldn't turn him off. I've tried everything! I clowned him in front of his boys and believe me boys aren't going to let you go that far. I mean it's not that I don't like him it's just that I never had a boyfriend before. I definitely don't want to go through this thing where I'm having boyfriend/girlfriend problems and dealing with all these chicken heads all over him.

You see, Corey is fine. His height was just right and he towered over me. He kept a clean, short hair cut, nice brown skin, cute little dimples, and ever so confident. I loved that about him. I wasn't sure what it was. I got weak for Corey at times, but knew our relationship wasn't like that. One thing was for sure…everyone thought he was good for me.

"So, ummm Anondi, what are we doing tonight dinner or a movie?" he asked.

"How about I'm hanging up, because I was on my way to take a nap? I'll call you and let you know when I wake up," I said sarcastically.

"Yeah you do that. Sleep on it and call me later sweet-heart."

"Alright Corey, I'll talk to you later."

I hung up thinking, Corey was a sweetheart for the most part. He'll make somebody happy one day I know.

I glanced at the clock, thinking wow, time sure does fly! Its three o'clock already. Before I knew it I was out cold.

It didn't take long for me to slip into a crazy dream. I was lying down in a grassy green field, for hours, which was fine, because I loved it. But what bothered me was that fact that I could really feel the rain on my clothes. I jumped up to find that Lauren was spraying a whole bottle of water from my *Mr. squirt me when I'm hot bottle.* We used that on hot summer days when we sat out back on my patio. It was a red spray bottle that really had *Mr. Squirt me when I'm hot* taped around it.

Lauren and I seemed to goof off all the time like that. I never figured out what possessed me to do that. But anyway, I jumped up to kill her. She knew I was going to go berserk, so she started to run. I had no real energy to chase her. I felt that excruciating pain in my head again as soon as I hopped to get up. As usual it was on the left side of my head. I grabbed my head and crawled back over to my bed with my head resting on the edge. Lauren saw that I wasn't feeling well so she came back over to check on me. She kneeled down next to me.

"Hey, you good? It's those headaches again, isn't it?" she asked almost sure of it. She moved my hands from my head.

"Yeah, it just caught me off guard that time. I'm cool L," I assured her.

"Girl, did you tell your dad that your head is still bothering you? You got to get that checked babes."

"I did go to get it checked. They simply gave me some pills for it. But they didn't find anything wrong."

I got up and sat on the bed.

"Well I beg to differ, because everyday you have headaches. What you going to do? Keep pacifying it with a drug that's not going to fix the problem? All it does is put to you out like a light."

"You're right. Look, just don't worry about it, L."

"Okay, but I really think you should look into this a lil' more before something serious happens. Go and get a second opinion," she said standing up.

I didn't even respond to it. Instead I just changed the subject. I looked out the window noticing that it was night time.

"Why are you so late? I thought you said you were coming earlier? It's clearly eight," I said looking at the clock, realizing I'd slept a long time.

"No special reason. Kevin and I just decided to spend a little more time. And girl…" Lauren smiled from ear to ear. I cut her short though.

"I don't even want to know any details, because I know that's where you are going with this. All I want to do is go downstairs, get me a pill, and go right back to sleep. No offense boo," I said straining to wink, because of the pain.

"I was just going to say we just chilled in his basement and watched movies. We got real caught up. We eventually fell asleep."

"So, you just had to get it out huh?" I said laughing.

"You know it. But look, you sit here. I'll go get your stuff. Lay down," she demanded.

"Yes, Mom," I said in a whiny voice.

I walked over to open the double doors to my bedroom balcony so that I could enjoy the night air. It always felt best during the night time hours. I enjoyed sitting outside to catch the breeze. I simply lit a candle to keep the bugs away. I hopped back in the bed with my dog on my heels as usual. I grabbed my laptop to check my Myspace page again.

MeMe wanted to watch the colors on the screen so she jumped up on me cuddling in my lap. Sometimes as crazy as it sounded, I believed that Me Me took on my mother's spirit when she died. It was like she always knew when something was wrong, and she tried with all her little doggy might to make it better. I loved that about her.

I had a ton of messages; one from Davon again. He wanted to know where was my favorite place to hang out. I told him St. Charles Mall, near my house.

"Here's your cranberry juice and your pill, Sick Betty," Lauren announced, climbing on the bed next to me.

"Thanks Ugly Betty," I said jokingly.

"Funny, but I'm far from ugly," Lauren shot back exposing her overbite, which I thought was kinda cute.

I starting reading Davon's response when Lauren peaked over my shoulder.

"Who might that be? He's cute, Nondi."

"Just someone who's real cool. He's my Myspace buddy. We write to each other sometimes, but that's it. Just cyber buddies," I said laughing.

"Oh good… cuz you know online dating is tacky."

We both laughed.

"He keeps asking to meet me, but I keep telling him no. It's like he doesn't get it. But he's cool I guess," I said, after reading his message.

I saw Lauren pick up my sidekick like she always did to see who called me. She knows I hated that crap, but she continues to do it anyway.

"Ummhmmm, three missed calls from Corey. Why you be trying to duck that boy? He's so sweet and cute," she said making me feel guilty.

"First off, I was sleep," I snapped. "And give me my phone." I tried to snatch my cell, but Lauren jerked back as I continued, "I don't try to duck him, I talked to him right before I took my nap. So talk what you know!" I was finally able to grab my phone from Lauren's grip, and put the laptop on my desk.

"Girl, please, you ignore his calls when you ain't sleep so be real! I mean I know you guys have been friends since you were kids. You might consider him like as a boyfriend, you dig. He's cute, funny, and smart. Besides, he's extra light-skinned like you like'em. The one you know can be the one you love," she said poking me in my stomach.

"I know that, but it's hard to go there with him. We've been strictly friends for so long. It's kind of dumb to go there now. Us together would be like Daphne and Fred from Scooby doo."

Lauren rolled her eyes. "To you it's dumb, but to me it would be the bomb. Fred and Daphne ended up together re-member. Ya'll been friends for more than ten years. He knows everything about you, has been there through everything, and not to mention is madly in love with you. You just don't see it, but the boy got love on his mind. He got a job, a car, and he is graduating in June, on time, from a top notch private school. How good can it get with this generation? I mean come on," she said cracking me up.

The funny part was that Lauren was totally right. I had nothing to say after that.

"See, when some other chicken head comes along and claims what should be yours, you'll see what I'm saying then. Girl, Corey loves you, and I know you love him too deep down inside."

All I could do was sit there and shake my head and think about her words. Everything she was saying was really true. I was ignoring him. I let my fear of being in a real rela-tionship cause me to miss out on my potential soul-mate. What if Corey is the one?

"By the way, I took one of your little drugs. I felt a lit-tle headache coming on myself," Lauren said rubbing her head.

"Girl, you're crazy! You always do that! Ain't nothing wrong with you. You're gonna get sick," I said pushing her.

We both laughed like crazy, then discussed Corey some more.

After about an hour and a half of talking about any and everything, I realized the pill had set in. We both sprawled out on the floor, talking out the side of our necks. The side affects of the pills should say guaranteed to knock you into partial oblivion. I mean we were talking about rainbows for God's sake.

"Hey, I just remembered the balcony door was still open. Can you get up and close it for me?"

"Why you open it, stupid, I can't even stand up straight," Lauren said staggering over to the window.

"Oh, and I guess you want me to go turn out the lights too. You are a trip I promise," looking at me from the balcony window.

"You know I love you, girl," I whispered.

I opened my phone one last time with the little bit of strength that I had. I sent Corey a little text that read:

```
I hit the Zzzz harda than I expected.
        Hit u up tomar
      4real. Ttyl. Nite.
```

I'd never sent Corey a text before bed. It was the least I could do since I didn't return his calls. I knew most likely he'd be knocking on my door tomorrow like always. My dad loves him though, so it wouldn't be a problem.

"Goodnight Corey!" Lauren sang. "See that's what I'm saying. He's the only boy you talk to… so you might as well," Lauren said, in an annoying childlike voice when she got back in the bed.

"Shut up ugly! You're so nosey."

"That is funny, but still far from me," she said.

We both sounded like we needed to shut up and go to

15

sleep.

"I hate when you take all the cover," I said pulling them from her.

"If you move this little silly looking dog then you could have some cover," she said giggling. "But you know you my boo, MeMe."

Me Me jumped off the bed and headed for her little bed in the corner. It's like she understood her.

"Now look you made her sad. Go to sleep. You're gonna give me another headache with your mouth."

Before I knew it, we were out like lights. Before I closed my eyes, I checked the time. It was 12:00 a.m. exactly. We did well. It was normally around five when we got to bed. I guess tonight was a good night

.

━━━━━━━━━

I could hear Lil Wayne's, *Lollipop* blaring in my ear. It interrupted my dream. I knew exactly who it was and I was going to kill him. "Not early in the morning! " I grunted with my eyes still slightly shut.

I opened my eyes to find him sitting at *my* desk on *my* laptop on *his* MySpace page. Seriously, what household do you know where the dad lets guys freely walk around his house? Especially when you have a teenage daughter.

I got up and bum rushed Corey so that he didn't have time to move. I wanted Lauren to help me, but I turned to see her still knocked out through all of the noise. That girl could sleep through the world ending if God would let her. Corey was jamming hard and had no idea I was coming up behind him to crash the party.

Slap! I hit the back of his neck with an open hand. "What are you doing fool? People are trying to sleep! Here you are making noise early in the morning!" I reached for him again, but missed. He nearly fell out of his chair.

"If you look at the little thing called a clock you would see that it's not morning anymore, it's afternoon. It's actually after one," Corey said grabbing his head.

"Oh, wow we must have slept the whole pill off. That's horrible I need to go take a bath. I missed half of the day!" I said frowning at the clock and classifying myself as a loser all at the same time.

"Yup you missed everything. I've been here since eleven. I'm proud of you, though. I didn't hear you snore not one time." He laughed. "But that thing over there, I don't know what she is anymore," he said pointing to Lauren.

All I could do was laugh. "Who let you in? My dad?"

"Yeah, I caught him just before he left for work. He was talking a hole in my head about my decision to go to law school. He wants me to work at his firm when I graduate. He kept going on, and on, and on….I'm like Mr…" I cut him off.

"Hey, that's my dad. Don't get smacked in the head again. You know he likes you. He's never had a son so he takes to you."

"Oh, so that means he would love it if I became his son- in- law, right?" Corey stood up and tried to put his arm around my shoulders.

"No, that's not what I meant," I said blocking him. "Go close my balcony door and get off my computer. There's personal stuff on there."

"Like what?" he asked when I pushed him out my chair.

"Like none of your business."

"By the way, who is the thug? I don't like how he's all in your business." Corey frowned.

I must have left my messages up last night from Davon.

"None of your business! That's why you're banned from my computer."

"You still need to be careful. I know I've never seen dude before. And I know you meet people all the time through sending friend request. Just be real chill with him," he said with concern.

"Thanks, but I'm straight. He's just a computer friend, that's all. I've never met him in person, and he doesn't know my number, or where I live."

"Keep it that way," he shot back, and turned around as I grabbed my towel off the back of the door.

I left out of the room to get my shower. It was routine for me to get up early so I could start my days off right. Every Saturday, I got up at nine, and preceded to my dance studio. My dad built it in the corner of the house for me when I first started dancing in middle school; my specialty, ballet and modern dance. My mom was also a good dancer as well. I guess I inherited the love for it from her. The space wasn't huge but nice and the perfect place to practice. I loved it there, because it's so peaceful, allowing things to flow freely.

After I got out the shower, I wiped the mirror clean of all the steam. I cracked the door open just a little to air it out. Unfortunately, I had to put on my under clothes in the bathroom, because of Corey. All of the steam made me feel sticky like I needed another shower. I grabbed a black band to put my hair in a bun. I hated wearing my hair in a ponytail, because Gabby always claimed it takes your hair out. However, my hair was long, and gets in the way of everything. I get the length from my mom and the texture from my dad. As I pulled my hair back, I realized how much I was starting to look like my mother, the same tan skin like I'd been sun bathing, dark long eye lashes, eyebrows, and jet black hair. We even rocked the same mole underneath our right eye.

I allowed my fingers to caress my skin when I felt a small knot on the side of my head near my temple. It wasn't very noticeable, but it was there. Maybe I hit my head on something while I was sleep and didn't know? Who knows... but it was strange.

I rushed back into the bedroom with my bathrobe on to find Corey sitting over top of Lauren trying to put something up her nose. *He was way too playful*, I thought to myself. Just before I could stop him, MeMe jumped up on the bed and started barking to warn Lauren. While he was trying to calm her barking down, Lauren opened her eyes ready for war. She still had what looked to be tissue stuck up her nose. Lauren hopped up and started chasing him all around the room. The two of them were running around screaming like crazy.

"I hate you! You play too much!" Lauren shouted.

When she caught Corey, she beat him down; humorously the dog was helping her. That's how it went down all the time, and I'd become so immune to it by now. I just put on my leotard and prepared myself to go down to the studio. I figured they would come down when they were done killing each other.

When I got into the studio and flicked the lights on, the cold air had me shivering. It usually warmed up once I changed the temperature, or started dancing. Either why I was freezing, and wished that I'd had a little more meat on my bones.

I'd managed to keep myself in shape by eating the right foods. I thought one hundred and twenty pounds was kinda good for a sixteen year- old at five feet four. I just had to stick to exercising through dance.

I turned on the CD that I'd created with all the songs that I liked to dance to. I did my normal warm up sessions. I stretched for about ten minutes, then started on some routines that we learned in class. I worked hard for nearly thirty minutes on previous learned dances. I always saved my freestyle

19

dance for last.

Finally, it was time. I did the Appeal by Kirk Franklin from his CD, Hero. That song always gave me serenity and peace. Just as I did my last drop at the end of the song, I heard my two knuckle heads clapping as I peaked at them over my bowed head. It scared me half to death, because I wasn't expecting them to come down just yet.

"Encore, encore!" Corey said, clapping ever so loudly along with L.

"Thank you," I replied snatching my towel and bottled water from him.

"You're welcome boo," he said winking at me.

We all sat in front of the large mirrors under the bar and just chilled out for a minute.

"So, what's on the agenda for today?" Lauren asked.

"The first thing we need to do is get your head checked out," Corey said. "Lauren and I have talked about it."

"That's the smartest thing you said in years," Lauren said, pushing Corey on the shoulder slightly.

"I'm fine," I announced. "I want to do something fun."

Let's go to the National Harbor. We can chill throughout the night. There's a lot to do there," Corey suggested.

"Alright that's cool. Your treat and we can't go until after five. My sister is coming," I announced proudly.

"I heard that my treat part. You better be glad I don't mind spending money on you, since you're not my girl. Or are you?"

"Yeah, you are a good dude. I will give you that. But you're stupid," Lauren said, and we laughed.

"Ha ha ha. You're so funny Lauren," Corey sarcastically.

We got up to go upstairs to the kitchen. The quick dance routine made me hungry, and in need of another shower. I grabbed a sandwich and some cranberry juice from the fridge and watched Lauren pig out like she hadn't eaten in years.

"I'm going up for another shower," I said biting into a juicy red apple. I grabbed my sidekick off the counter and saw that I had one missed call. It was the same number that texted me after school yesterday. Maybe they got the wrong person again. I thought about calling the number back but then decided against it.

By the time I got out of the shower, and threw on my Apple Bottom jeans and matching denim top it was near 5 o'clock. I knew my sister would be arriving at any moment. I couldn't wait to see her and hear what it is she had to tell me. Me, Corey, and Lauren sat around my room goofing off and talking crazy. We searched all over MySpace, Facebook, and Youtube laughing and listening to music. We eventually moved from my bedroom to sitting in our usual spot on my balcony. The breeze always felt so good. After a while I heard the doorbell ring. I stopped everything I was doing, and rushed to see who was at the door. I knew it was my sister.

"Gosh ugly!" Lauren shouted after I trampled all over them.

I opened the door to see Gabby standing there. The first thing she said was, "Nondi!"

She sounded just like she did when we were kids. We hugged so tightly, then screamed and laughed all the way into the house. While hugging her I felt something hard and big poking my stomach. I let go to get a good look at her.

"OMG, Gabby you're so beautiful.... and pregnant!" I said in a tone that said wow!

"Well, this is it," she said, barely smiling, with her hands rubbing her stomach.

"I mean like how did you...I mean... I know how...but did you tell Daddy!" I asked loss for words.

"Well, actually... no I didn't. I was sort of going to tell him tonight," she responded, as we sat down on one of the high chairs in the kitchen.

"I guess this is what you had to tell me?"

"No, Nondi, this is like showing you, but there is more. I'm getting married too. In three months," she said flashing her engagement ring.

"Okay, that's cool too. But I thought we vowed to just wait to get married for all this," I said pointing to her stomach.

"I know, but I fell in love and you know things happen. But promise me you won't give it up yet. You're too young. Besides, somebody gotta keep it together," she said giggling.

"Trust me, I'm good. I'm not interested in having a baby or a husband right now." I put my hand on my hips and crinkled my brows. "Are you ready for all this, Gabby? Like who is this guy? Is he here? I want to meet him!" I said excitedly.

"Well, I'm here alone. Michael is back in New York with his family. He's doing the same thing I'm doing, telling the news," she said. "So like how do you feel Nondi? You don't hate me do you?" she asked, with an unsure look on her face.

"Gabby, I love you and I'm excited for you. You know I will support you no matter what." I shot her a fake smile. "But I am worried about Dad. You know how much it meant to him for you to finish college."

"Wait, who said I wasn't gonna finish college? I will eventually finish. I know he'll be upset but I'm twenty years old. He should understand, and if not I'll just have to deal with whatever he says."

I wore a sour look on my face but cut the conversation short. I heard Corey and Lauren coming down to see my sister. They all entered the kitchen and hugged Gabby tightly. I waited to see if either of them noticed she was pregnant. They either didn't pay attention, or wanted to ignore the situation.

So did I, but I couldn't help but think what my dad

was going to say about Gabby. He'd always spoken so highly of Gabby and even at times looked down on others for their faults. I imagined how that conversation was going to go when he saw her. I guess that's just a bridge we'd all have to cross when we got there. Luckily for Gabby, Dad said he'd be pulling an all nighter at his firm, so that would give us time for peace.

"Hey, Gabby, we were thinking about going out to the Harbor tonight. You feel up to it?" I asked.

"Yeah, why not. Let's go have some fun. I had a long trip here, why not take a load off," she responded.

Corey started jiggling his keys. "Okay cool, lets go now before it gets too late. Now it's still my treat but if we stay in here another five minutes I'm changing my mind," he announced.

"Alright, well let's go. We wouldn't want you to do that," Lauren said opening the door, leading us all out to Corey's Lexus truck.

We got to the Harbor around 6 p.m. We picked up some grub and ate ice cream at Ben and Jerry's. We really had a lot of fun. I knew it was only going to be a matter of time before one of my headaches showed up to haunt me. On the way to the car, I felt a sharp pain zip through my head. I had to bend down to brace myself for the pain.

"Nondi, you okay?" Gabby asked.

"No, she's not. It's those stupid headaches again. Maybe you can get her to go back to the doctor to get it checked," Lauren intervened.

"How many times am I going to tell you? I went and it's all good. It was just a quick sharp pain. I'll just take my pill when I get home," I said standing up.

I saw Corey watching me with a somber face. I didn't need a pity party.

"Nondi, I really want to talk to your dad about this,"

Corey said, grabbing me by the arm.

"Look, look I told you I'm alright would you guys please just stop!" I pleaded with them all. This is starting to annoy me."

"Okay everybody, chill out!" Gabby added. "Let's just get her home. We'll take care of it when we get there."

As we were walking to the car, I got a text on my phone from a number I didn't know again. The text was blank though. I turned around and a car went flying past us. It almost swiped Corey, but he was about two seconds short. Everybody started yelling at the unknown driver.

I got a good look at the car as it slowed and turned back around the lot. When I noticed that it was the same black Crown Vic with the tinted windows, that I'd seen before. My eyes almost popped out of my head.

"Watch where you're going fool!" Lauren yelled.

After that, everybody brushed it off and got in the car. They concluded that it was just some random idiot driving crazy. I wasn't convinced…but had other issues to worry about at that moment. At least my sister was okay though.

On our way out of the lot the same foolish driver pulled in front of us, about six yards away, then stopped abruptly. We tried to get a good look at him, but he drove off rapidly, screeching his tires in the process.

"Okay, now that was weird," Corey said, rushing toward the highway.

We got to our neighborhood within twenty minutes flat. Corey dropped us off and made sure we got in the house safely. I was just so ready to go to bed. , but I just couldn't get that black car out of my mind. I wondered who it could've been and why they would scare us like that. I didn't know anybody with a car like that. It was bothering me, because two times in one weekend, I'd seen it, then all the unknown numbers. I had that on my mind and a lot of other things, especially Gabby's situation. I really wanted my sister to finish college.

Once inside the house, I realized my dad hadn't gotten home just yet. It was almost midnight. I guess that was a good thing. Now, Gabrielle could get off her feet peacefully and get some rest. I headed to change my clothes and said goodnight to my sister. She gave me everything I needed as far as nursing my headache.

It seemed as if only a few minutes had passed and I was in bed with the covers pulled up to my neck. I looked at my cell phone beneath the covers to check my messages. That was the only light in the room. I had two text messages from my favorite folks; Corey and Lauren. Corey's message read, "Call me" and Lauren told me she loved me. I responded to Lauren and decided to call Corey. He seemed to be growing on me.

"Hey boo. What you doing?" he asked answering the phone.

For some reason it didn't bother me. "Nothing, just lying in the bed. What's up with you?"

"Nothing. Just thinking about you and everything you do," he said in a sensual tone. "I need to talk to you about something."

"Corey…" I whined knowing exactly where he was going with the conversation.

"What? I mean why you can't just accept somebody being nice to you?" he said obviously annoyed. What if I want to be serious for once? What if I want to be truthful and really tell you what's on my mind?"

I got completely silent.

He continued. "I love you Anondi. I always have, ever since the first day I met you. We were kids but you know…I've never been able to shake you. Now what do you have to say?"

25

I was certainly loss for words. I had no idea what to say. All I could say to him was exactly what I was thinking.

"I don't know what to say Corey." I really wanted to say it back but I was unsure if I meant it.

"Don't say anything. Just say you'll give us a try, please.

I paused then breathed heavily.

"What else can I do to prove to you that I want to be more than just your annoying friend? I want to be the one who you talk to every night until you fall asleep, and the one you share everything with. Just say you'll try," he asked again in the most serious and sincere way ever.

I took another second to pause. I thought deeply and reflected back on everything he'd just said. It was all true and I couldn't argue with him at all.

"Okay," shot from my mouth. I didn't even think about it.

Corey obviously didn't understand what I meant. "What? See I knew you would make me feel like a fool," he said sounding defeated.

"Corey, I'm saying okay to us. Okay I'll try us."

"Oh," he responded in shock.

"Yes, now let's do us," I said to smooth out the awk-wardness.

We talked on the phone as usual about any and every-thing for hours. It was beautiful, and I felt good about it too. I didn't take him as joke, or laugh at any of the dumb things he said. Instead, I appreciated his words. I was definitely antici-pating seeing him when I woke up the next morning.

We talked until 1a.m. when Corey got sleepy. For some reason, I couldn't sleep. I was still thinking about that car. I was also thinking about that suspicious blank text I got before I got in the car. This was getting way too spooky. Maybe it was just coincidental.

I got online when I got off the phone with Corey. I started changing up my page, and uploading pictures of me and Corey. I even changed my profile from single to taken. I didn't know what time of the morning it was when I got off. I had to go to the bathroom badly. On the way, I saw my Dad in Gabby's room. He was sitting on the side of the bed, with his hands pressed against his forehead while she lay under the covers. I knew it was impossible for him to notice our big surprise. Considering the fact that they were not arguing, I take it he doesn't know yet. I quietly walked over to the door, deciding to ease drop. It was dead wrong but I wanted to hear what they were talking about.

"Yeah Dad, it was a long drive. I'm so exhausted," Gabrielle was saying while yawning.

"I know Sweet Pea, just get some rest. I'm getting ready to leave you alone. I was thinking since I haven't been able to spend any time with you or Anondi we can do some catching up. So how about tonight at eight we do dinner?"

"Sure why not, I don't have anything to do."

"Okay, well I'll be working until seven. By the time I get across town it'll be eight so it all works."

"Great. We'll just meet you there," Gabby confirmed.

"Sweet Pea go back to bed," he said, kissing her cheek.

He was moving too fast for me to even run and fake like I wasn't listening. I just pretended like I was coming to say hello to him.

"Oh, hi, Daddy… just on my way to the bathroom," I said in a slick voice.

"Umm, huh, it's 3 a.m., go back to bed baby girl."

"You're right," I said hugging him.

I rushed inside of Gabby's room and used her bathroom. When I came out she was looking at me like I was crazy.

"What? I had to pee," My arms spread widely apart.

"You were being nosey too."

"Well, yes I was. I thought I was going to wake up to another addition of 'My Dad killed my sister'. But I see he didn't pay it any mind right?" I said rubbing her little belly.

"Well I'm glad that gives me time to prepare myself for him and his reaction. Dinner was definitely a good idea, because that way he won't zap out too much in front of the public," she said laughing.

"I know, right. He'll be okay. He can't change anything. He's just going to have to deal with it. You're not a little kid anymore."

"You're right. I pray he understands. If he doesn't he will one day," she said looking down at her stomach.

"Auntie says he better, because you're definitely going to be something special," I said, in a playful tone while talking to the baby. "This daddy I got to meet too."

"You'll hear all about him later on today. Oh yeah, and Nondi... I'm sorry for not telling you."

"It's okay, but you're definitely going to pay once you drop this load ugly," I said poking her.

"Yeah right. I love you big head. I'm tired."

"I love you too... and ummm... I got a boo," I said walking out the door.

"Who? I'll kill him," she said.

"Corey," I said winking my eye while peaking my head back in the doorway.

I could hear her whispering as loud as she could.

"Wait, I knew it, and since when?"

I just said, "Tomorrow! You'll hear about it all tomorrow!"

I got to the room and she sent me a text saying

You betta. I'm proud of u.
He's a good choice.

I replied back *"psycho"*.

I had one unread message from yet another unknown number. It read:

Not yesterday…then today. I can't wait."

"Who is this!" I typed back. It was starting to scare me. I didn't get an answer. I just snuggled underneath the covers and prayed as I fell asleep.

═══════════

Ten o'clock had rolled around by the time I'd gotten up the next morning. I felt as if I hadn't slept in days. I felt like a two-headed monster. Part of me was feeling good about my new start with Corey, while the other side of me was still shaken up about the Crown Vic. But I didn't want to make too much of it. So, I did my daily routine to get my mind off of things.

I danced for maybe an hour longer than usual. Lauren showed up around one, and Corey showed up about two. As usual, we sat out on my balcony. When Lauren noticed the way Corey and I were acting, she almost lost her breath.

She wanted every single, solitary detail about everything that led to our decision to give dating a try. During the day Lauren would make crazy comments about us, then she and Corey would continue with their usual spats like Pam and Martin. But she was really extra. It was different from our usual hang out, but my mother had always said, change is good.

Every five minutes I kept looking at the passing traffic and checking my phone. No one noticed me being uneasy though. After a while Lauren left to go meet Kevin at the mall, so it was just me and Corey. I was very reluctant to tell him about that text message. I just didn't want to be too dramatic. I didn't want to think about it.

Seven rolled around and I started preparing to meet Dad.

The restaurant he picked was Valentino's. I wanted to mimic my sister's clothes on our dinner date so we both wore spaghetti strapped dresses that flared out at the bottom. I wore my Betsy Johnson big ring and my juicy couture bracelet and matching necklace. I wet my hair during my second shower of the day into a stylish, curly bush. Of course Corey watched the whole process. Even when I was putting on mascara he watched.

"So, this is what you do to get ready to go just about anywhere, huh?"

"This is why it takes us so long; we come out looking like this," I said turning around to show off my figure.

Corey shook his head with delight as he watched me put on my perfume and apply more lip gloss.

"Are you sure you're just going out with your Dad? You're getting extra cute. I don't have to tag along do I?" he said hugging me from behind.

"No, you don't. It's just us," Gabby interrupted while she wobbled into the room.

"Come on now Corey, we have to go," I said, moving his arms away from my waist. It was clear Corey didn't want to take things slowly. I did. "Calm down," I told him. "I gotta get used to this." I turned on a sour face and headed to the front door.

When Gabby smiled at me, I noticed we had the same curly bush. But it was sort of cute though despite the fact we looked exactly alike. I just didn't have the belly to match. Shortly after 8pm we pulled up to Valentino's. That was just like my dad to pick something that we'd never even heard of. I would have been alright just eating at the Outback Steakhouse.

Fortunately he had made reservations. Although the restaurant seemed to be packed, we were seated amongst the crowd, and ordered a few drinks; but declined on ordering any food until my Dad showed up. It was around eight-fifteen when I looked up and saw him approaching the table.

"I'm sorry I'm late girls I had to change my clothes," he said as he kissed both of us on our foreheads.

"It's alright. We haven't been waiting that long," I assured him.

The waiter rushed over and took his drink order. It was crazy how he talked so proper. He asked us about appetizers and promised to come back shortly to take our food order. My Dad snapped his fingers out of the blue and ordered his old faithful, Merlot.

For a while we shared small talk about almost everything that had occurred in all of our lives over the last few months. Dad told us about his firm and his last few cases that had him locked down. I talked about school, dancing, and Corey. Dad didn't seem surprised about me and Corey. In fact, he told me he loved Corey and trusted him wholeheartedly with his daughter. He ended with, "But I gotta keep a close watch on you guys now."

We all laughed for several seconds at his comment, but when it got to Gabrielle things got a little awkward.

"Well sweetie, how does it feel to be in your third year of college?" He reared back in his seat. "I'm so proud of you. So tell me how New York life been treating you?" he asked.

I could see nervousness in Gabby's eyes as my father analyzed them

"Well daddy you know the same ole' long classes and mile high work. I did find a good job and an apartment though," she said, then shot him a half of a smile.

I was ready to kill her. She always seemed to leave the pregnancy part out. She did it to me first, and now my dad.

"Wow sweetie, that's great I didn't know that. I'm a proud Dad… I can say that. Now let me ask you, have you found that special someone? Has anyone tried to sweep you off your feet?" he asked rubbing her right hand.

I sure knew the answer to that question. Gabby got even more nervous to the point where I could feel her leg shaking.

"That's something I've been meaning to talk to you about Dad. I'm engaged," she said bringing her left hand to the top of the table.

He paused for a second, then grabbed her hand.

At first, he simply twitched in his seat, then his face transformed into a frown. "Wow sweetheart, how could you keep something like this from me?" He crossed his arms just as his frown deepened. "I mean are you ready for this? I haven't met the guy," he said on the peak of being rattled.

"Well, Dad, before you go on, there's more. You haven't really seen me except the night I was in bed. Of course now, I'm sitting down."

"And…" he snarled.

Gabby scooted her chair back for my father to get a good look. "Not only am I getting married…you're going to be a grandfather," she said as she stood up to show her growing belly.

At one point I could see the veins in my father's forehead almost pop completely out. He was as red as an Iroquois Indian.

"Dad, calm down. We can talk rational about this," I said rubbing his arm. Ironically, the waiter showed up to take our order.

"Are we all ready to order?" he asked sensing there was trouble.

"Not right now. Can you give us a minute," I replied as he nodded in compliance.

My dad never looked his way. He was fuming.

"What on earth were you thinking Gabrielle Symone Wade! How could you make such a poor decision? You come from a household where you were born to a husband and a wife. Now I suspect that's how you got your new place, your estranged fiancé that no one ever knew about. I bet you two aren't even getting married," he said, causing a scene. He was deep into Gabby's face, almost nose to nose.

"Dad can you calm down people are looking," I said.

"I want you to listen and watch," he said to me. "Is this the example you want to show your younger sister? That it's cool to have babies out of wedlock?"

He went on and on. I kept saying his name trying to get him to stop but he wouldn't. Eventually, Gabby started to crying and I was getting fed up. She kept trying to tell him how she was grown. She wanted him to understand, but he was just being a butt hole. It really started to stress me out and I could feel myself getting so angry at him. The waiter was on his way back.

"Sir, could you all keep it down just a little, you're causing a bit of a distraction," he said in the nicest way possible, then he left. So I figured it was my time to step in.

"Dad look, you need to calm down. No disrespect, but this is your daughter. Listen to yourself and look at her crying. She needs your support and she doesn't have it at all. If mom were here, do you think she would have reacted this way? No, she would embrace Gabby and talk to her to fix this." I stopped and looked my dad deep into his eyes. "Gabby *will* be married by the time the baby is born. You want me to sit here and listen but believe me I know right from wrong! I'm not sexually active, and I'm not having any babies until I'm married! "

Everyone was silent at that point. I had the floor and demanded attention. I started to gather my things to prepare myself to leave. Gabrielle did the same thinking she was coming along.

"No, you stay here, I'm leaving. You two need to talk

and have dinner as a father and daughter would. Eat, and come to some sort of resolution." I leaned to kiss them both on the cheek. "Dad, bring Gabby home with you. I love you both… remember, you never know what could happen to any of us. We are all we have. Try to find a way to get over this." I waved like a happy schoolgirl, but deep inside I was worried as my feet walked uneasily out of the restaurant.

On the way to the car, I pulled out my sidekick and asked Corey to meet me at the house. My phone was dying with only a tiny bit of charge remaining. I really needed someone to talk to, so I kept the conversation brief, focusing on the fact that he needed to come right away. I honestly didn't think that my dad would act out in a public restaurant like that.

When I drove into the neighborhood, I saw that Corey hadn't left home yet. He lived on the first street in Simmons Estates. I thought about stopping at his house until something inside of me said no, he would show up soon.

When I pulled into my driveway, I saw a light skinned guy dressed in all black talking on a cell phone. His face wasn't too visible, mostly because of the baseball cap he wore. He was sitting on the side walk across from the neighborhood field just ten yards from my house. The field was a huge grassy area where everyone took their pets and children to play, yet he had neither. He was sitting with his head downward like his conversation wasn't going well.

All I could think about was how everybody's life seemed to have challenges. Then it hit me. I looked out my rearview mirror and saw that black Crown Vic to my right. My focus changed instantly. I looked back toward the field and noticed the light skinned guy had disappeared. Instantly, my heart began to race. So much had gone on, I didn't know what to think. I was stuck. I started sweating instantly. I didn't know if I should get out, or call somebody. I pulled out my phone to call Corey but it was dead.

I figured if I could at least get inside the house, I could call the police. I got out of the car and started running toward my house at top speed. I looked back when I reached the door. I heard him call my name. When I saw this guy coming toward me he looked familiar. He was about six feet tall and slim. When he got closer, I saw that it was Davon, my Myspace friend. I was sure my expression showed my confusion. How did he know where I lived?

"Oh, wow, you are even prettier in person," he said walking through my yard directly up to me. He looked much older than nineteen, as he'd quoted on is Myspace profile. I was shaking so hard he had to have known. I was praying that Corey would hurry.

"What are you doing here? How did you know where I lived?" I asked leaning on the front door.

He looked crazy in the face, and his tattoos alongside his neck made me even more uncomfortable.

"I looked under your school name and found you. Such an essential element on the space," he said being sarcastic. He started moving closer to me. Step by step he frowned and developed a sadistic grimace.

"I suggest you leave now! I'm going to call the police!" I said shouted, pointing to him.

"Wow, don't you think that's a bit much? I just want us to go for a ride. You owe me that. Those text and internet relationships get boring. Don't you think?" he said moving closer.

"I'm not going anywhere with you Davon! Now just leave!"

"I didn't come all this way for nothing. So you better give in or I'ma just have to force you," he said getting angry.

"You are not going to put your hands on me!" I shouted as I looked to my left and right for an escape.

Before I knew it, he'd grabbed me and threw me over

his shoulders. All I could do was scream! I called out, somebody! Anybody! Help!"

I fought him hard, yet nothing fazed him. And his strength seemed to overpower me. The more he stepped toward his car, the more I squirmed.

Next thing I knew, I heard a car pull up. I saw Corey running toward Davon and me. I was like he heard me calling for him. "Corey, help!"

Before I knew it my dad had driven up on the scene and was outta his car like a character on Law and Order. They started beating Davon down instantly.

I ran to Gabby, fell into her arms, and allowed my tears to flow. She had already called the police and they were on the way. Luckily, my dad was able to pin Davon down to the ground with Corey's help. Within minutes a police car was on the scene. I breathed heavily while we watched as the two men jumped from the car and took hold of Davon. He was handcuffed and shoved into the car all within seconds.

It turned out that Davon wasn't Davon at all. He was a registered sex offender that the authorities had been looking for. He was actually twenty-five years old. I just didn't understand why he'd chosen me. I never gave him the impression that I wanted him. After the police talked to me and got all his info we all retreated into the house. I already knew my dad was going to go off.

"No more Myspace in this house. I promise you! How smart were you being sweetheart? Looking at the situation, it wasn't smart at all. This crap was brought to my home," he said pacing the floor.

I sat in the plush, leather chair in front of him.

"Just talk to Corey when you're lonely. Myspace might seem like the new thing, but you've got to be careful. People are crazy out here!"

"Dad, I'm sorry. I didn't know that he would try to find

me," I cried.

"I know sweetheart but the bottom line is…." he continued but I lost focus. I felt the worse pain in my head. It was stronger than before. I needed to get some pills fast, and a place to lay down.

"Are you okay, Nondi?" Gabby asked when she saw me bend my head down into my lap.

"Babe you alright? Do I need to get you something?" Corey cosigned.

"No, I'm fine. I just need to go get my pills and something to drink. I'll be okay." I stood up to go into the kitchen. My Dad was still going on and on as usual.

"Dad, we've been through enough tonight. Let's just sleep on it and deal with it tomorrow. It's late," Gabby said.

As I was walking toward my room, I could feel my head throbbing to the point where I couldn't even see. My legs started to stagger as well. The next thing I knew, I fell to the ground, hitting my head really hard in the process.

I strained to open and close my eyes. With each try my motions picked up the pace a bit. I could feel how heavy my lids were. I looked up at the ceiling and it was totally different from my room ceiling. I felt like I had taken a whole bottle of those Percocets. When I built up enough strength to look around, I saw Corey, Gabby, Lauren, and my Dad all coming toward my hospital bed. I heard the machines beeping but unsure why I had been admitted. So my first instinct was to panic and that's what I did.

"Daddy," I moaned with a fearful look.

"Calm down, baby girl its okay. You're alright, we are here." My Dad followed the doctor toward my bed.

"Ms. Anondi, my name is Dr. Joy. I'm going to be car-ing for you during your stay here at Grace Memorial. Can you remember anything that has happened to you tonight?" she asked in a loud voice that made my head hurt.

"Noooooooooo," I dragged. All I could remember was hitting my head on the ground really hard."

"Well you should really thank your family here. If someone hadn't been there during your seizure you would have been worse off," she said rubbing my shoulders.

"Seizure?" I repeated.

"Yes, Anondi. Can I get everyone to leave the room except Mr. Wade?" the doctor turned to ask everyone. They all agreed with head nods and left the room headed for the waiting area.

"Okay, Mr. Wade, the neurologist examined your daughter which is procedure whenever a seizure occurs. He found that she has a marble sized cancerous cyst that has been enlarging itself around the temple area of your daughter's head. Now, it's nothing to worry about, because it can be removed, but what I will say is that she has to get the procedure done as soon as possible. It has been enlarging itself every day. Luckily, we caught it in time," she ended.

I was definitely loss for words. Instantly, I realized the importance of going to doctors and getting second opinions. "This explains the headaches and the knot I felt on my head," I told my dad.

Now, I felt dumb for not listening to Lauren when she said I needed to be checked again. How could the doctors over look something like this? I thought to myself. I just instantly started to cry from fear. Cancer killed my mom. And if I hadn't fainted, I could've been worse off. I just don't know why this had to happen to me.

I stared frightfully as my father and the doctor set up my surgery. It was scheduled for 4 a.m. which was three hours away. I was so afraid just thinking about going under the knife, and having that ugly scare on the side of my head for the rest of my life. But that should've been the least of my worries.

Soon, everybody came in to hug me. I apologized to Lauren for not listening to her medical advice, and thanked Corey for being so brave.

I was wheeled out of the room with my hurt beating like a drum. The doctors talked to me on the way to ICU, telling me to relax, and that I would be given anesthesia shortly.

After being given the drug, the surgeon told me to count to one hundred, but I never even got to ten. The next thing I knew everything became blurry, then black... I was out.

Ten Days Later

After five whole days of white sheets, beeping sounds, and nurses waking me up every twenty minutes, I was finally ready to leave Grace Memorial. I can truly say that I'd learned a lot. God has a funny way of showing you how much he cares. If I had not had that seizure, I would've still been having the same problems, and not doing anything to correct the problem. He also protects you even when you think you don't need it. I would've never known about Davon, or the potential dangers of internet stalkers.

My dad and I pulled up to the house to find a yard full of cars. There was a sign that read "Welcome home baby girl!"

"Daddy you didn't?"

"Yes, I did. Sweetie, I could've lost you twice. I wouldn't be able to live without you. So come on, let's celebrate," he said as he opened my door and took me inside the house. I saw some of my family members, my old dance teachers, and my three favorite people; Lauren, Gabby, and

Corey. I was so excited, and glad to be home around the people I loved most. I saw that my future brother in law was there and I looked forward to getting to know him.

I whispered to Gabby, "He's cute, girl."

She smiled…I did too. I thought about how my father had pushed his feelings aside to be there for my sister and the baby. Everything seemed to be back to normal. I heard he'd even taken time off of work over the past few days. And said he would do the same in November when the baby was born.

"Hey, beautiful," Corey said coming up behind me. "I bet your mom is proud of you." He grinned, then rubbed my shoulders supportively.

"Yeah, she'll be happy to know I'm going to delete my Myspace page and start over. I'll have all private settings and no one can be my friend unless they know my last name or email. I thought about it all deeply…it's not Myspace that's bad, it's the people who abuse it."

I kissed Corey on the cheek.

"What did I do to deserve that?"

"Go with me down to the studio," I pleaded.

I was beginning my new life off right. Although we had a full house, I was on my way to take a look at my dance studio. I'd missed dancing so much. When we got down the steps, I took one look at myself in the mirror, pulled my hair back in my old faithful bun, and I saw that my little scare wasn't that bad after all.

"It looks good," Corey said.

I smiled. "I know…it's a sign of my testimony."

HE DOES IT ONCE-HE'LL DO IT AGAIN

by Iman Smallwood

Big Joe watched from the window, with a squinted eye as the young looking hoodlum approached his front door. Quickly, he rose from his outdated leather Lazy Boy, with an evil expression on his face.

"I got it, Uncle Joe!" Sonya shouted from upstairs as she skipped a few stairs trying to make it down to the front door.

Her ponytail shook from side to side as she picked up the pace.

"Who the heck is it?" he asked.

"I got it!"

"I didn't ask you that," he said, grabbing the knob on the door.

Sonya looked up at her muscular uncle who stood at least 2 feet over her petite frame. "He's just a friend," she said innocently. "I'll go out on the front porch." Her eyes begged for permission.

"Okay, watch yourself," he said, in his deep, baritone voice. "You're only fifteen, so there's no dating just yet. Besides, I know nothing about this guy. He from 'round here?"

"Umm…"

"Never mind," Big Joe responded, as he cracked the door open slightly. "Young man, what's your name?" he asked giving the youngster direct eye contact.

"Scoop," he answered in an unfriendly tone, then quickly turned away. Scoop flipped his hoodie onto his head, and stood with his hands deep into his pockets. His expression showed that he was tired of waiting for Sonya to come out onto the porch. He wasn't even fazed when Joe shot him a disapproving look at his sagging jeans.

"Son, what's your real name? And hurry up before I ask you for some I.D."

"Craig…Craig Jackson," he answered with a smirk.

"Well, Craig Jackson, my niece doesn't date. So don't get too comfortable with comin' 'round here making the property value go down in my neighborhood."

Sonya's jaw was still hanging low when her uncle walked away. She knew Uncle Joe was old school and didn't care if he gave her new friend a piece of his mind. He felt like every young teen should be taught by every adult he or she came in contact with, just like when he was young. Finally, Sonya opened the door just enough to slide out, and smiled at Scoop, hoping that her uncle hadn't ruined her chances with him.

"He didn't really mean that," Sonya said with embarrassment. "He'll be a lot nicer once he gets to know you."

"What? You think I care?" Scoop hunched his shoulders and made sure his frown looked tough. "I'on care about that old cat. I'm just tryin' to get wit' you."

Scoop managed to let a smile creep from the side of his lips. Sonya immediately returned the smile. It was obvious that she had a deep crush; one that her uncle would most definitely try to end when he found out that Scoop was seventeen, and still in the ninth grade.

"So, when we goin' out?" he asked.

"Aahh…"

"Lemme guess. You can't."

Sonya giggled. "I can surely try to make it happen. Let me find out when the coast will be clear, and I'll let you know."

"Yo, you live like you locked down 'round this camp." He frowned. "You got a cell phone?"

"Nah… I'm supposed to be getting one for my birthday." She lied.

"Well, from now on you call me. I'on know 'bout callin' you. I'm just not feelin' callin' your house."

"Oh, don't worry about that," Sonya said with confidence.

"Ummm…don't worry? Yeah, right," Scoop said sarcastically. "Let's link up for your birthday."

"I'd like that."

Sonya smiled showing off her brand new set of braces, just as Scoop bent down pretending to mess with his Timberland boots. He turned toward the window to see if Big Joe was watching. The curtains continued to move slightly making him feel uneasy about being there.

"Look here, I gotta go," he said standing. "I'll see you at school tomorrow. You think a brotha can get a kiss?"

Sonya blushed. Her entire honey colored face turned pale, and her cheeks resembled a reddish plum. "That might not be a good idea," she said, wishing that she could. Scoop was extremely attractive, and reminded Sonya of Bow Wow, just a rough neck version. Even the small twist he'd recently gotten in his hair added to his bad boy style.

"Holla," he said walking off the porch.

"Until then," she responded, still smiling. She played with a few strands of her hair with one hand while she continued waving with the other until Scoop was out of sight.

The moment Sonya entered the house, she was face-to-face with Uncle Joe. He stood at the door, with his arms crossed resembling Sonya's late father Jim, Joe's brother. Sonya's mother and father had been dead for nearly four years, leaving Big Joe and his wife to take care of Sonya and her little sister, Angel. The girls were grateful that they had relatives who really cared for them, but wanted just a little bit of freedom. Living in the Carrington house was like being locked down at a prison camp. Joe always repeated his favorite line, "*I'm from the old school, I know what's up. I'm just trying to protect you.*"

Big Joe never revealed his real age, but appeared to be in his late forties. He did his best to portray an upstanding image for the girls, but word has it that he'd dabbled into the bad life in his early years himself. A family member once slipped up and told Sonya that Big Joe used to be a member of the Supreme Gang, a gang known for committing countless murders, and several beat-downs in Brooklyn back in the day. So, for Sonya, she was tired of seeing him act like he'd never done anything wrong.

"Why would you embarrass me like that?" she whined. "You think everybody is a gang banger!"

"No, I don't. I just know the look. I can smell'em too," he said seriously. "That boy don't look like he got nothing good on his mind. He probably don't take school seriously, and definitely don't have no manners." He pointed at Sonya as if she were in trouble. "If he had any sense, he would've pretended to be a pleasant guy the moment I started talking to him. Instead, he couldn't even look me in the eye."

"He was probably scared," Sonya shouted, in Scoop's defense.

"You gotta be kidding me. That youngster probably had his glock down in his shoe. Remember, you're only fifteen years old Sonya!"

"Ten days away from being sixteen!" she shouted back.

"So what! I've got shoes older than you. Whatcha think about that!"

Sonya didn't respond. She jetted upstairs to her room, slammed the door, and pressed her head deep into her pillow.

She cried thinking about her mother. She wondered if she were alive would she be allowed to date. Would her mother allow her father, uncle, or whomever, torture her friends?

Sonya lifted her mattress to write the day's events in her journal, when she came across a list her uncle had given her last year on her fifteenth birthday. The title-More Tip's From Uncle Joe. (1). Never, lower your standards when interested in a mate. She smiled inside looking at his comment in parenthesis- *some little knuckle-headed boy*. Just because you may think they're cute on the outside, doesn't mean they're any good on the inside. (2). A boy will always show whether he's interested in you, or what's between your legs by the way he respects other females in general. Watch him closely... (3) The moment a male disrespects you, and you allow it... things will never change; but don't worry. I'll have my shotgun ready.

Sonya quickly closed the book. She couldn't take it anymore. Uncle Joe had given her countless tips on the do's and don'ts when dealing with boys. Quite frankly, she'd heard enough.

"I've gotta get outta here," she screamed as she pressed her head back into the pillow. "I'm about to be sixteen, and in jail! Somebody help me!"

Sonya cried herself to sleep.

———————

Several days later, Sonya couldn't fight off the urge to see Scoop any longer. Shortly after school let out, Sonya, Damo, and Brittany walked down Marshall street, just two blocks over from Greenbriar High school. Sonya had begged her two best friends for days to accompany her near Scoop's hang out. This was the only way she'd be able to spend a little time with him without her uncle knowing about it.

Scoop hadn't been to school all week, but talked to Sonya over the phone a few times. He claimed he had work to do, and school wasn't in the picture for now. Sonya thought it was strange, but wanted to be in his presence no matter what.

The plan was set, even though Brittany didn't like it one bit. She was a prissy teen, and only went after the boys at school who seemed to have it going on. As far as she was concerned, Scoop was dirty, and hung out with the wrong crowd. She and Sonya had been friends for three years, so she made an exception and walked with her toward Shephard's Terrace.

The moment they rolled into the neighborhood, Damo became frightened. "You sure about this Sonya?" he asked, in his light voice.

"I'm sure," Sonya answered cheerfully.

"Everything frightens you, Damo. For a boy, you've been sheltered too much."

"Now we've been friends for a long time, and you've never said that before. Now all of a sudden you got your little bad boy boyfriend who just happens to hang out in thuggish neighborhoods, and I'm sheltered! Whatever! I'm smart. We should go. Does he even know you're coming?"

"Scoop told me to come. So c'mon."

Although Sonya spoke with confidence, her mind said something different. Shephard's Terrace was known to be a criminal's sanctuary. The most common drug deals and gun battles took place there. Not even the toddlers were supervised. They often played into the wee hours of the night like it was two o'clock in the afternoon.

Feeling the stares, Sonya clenched the straps on her backpack as she looked for Scoop. Thugs sat on cars shouting in foul language, while crack-heads walked the cul-de-sac.

Damo looked back and noticed there was one way in-and one way out. "Sonya, I know you wanna see this dude, but I'm 'bout to leave."

"No…," she said grabbing his sleeve. "There's Scoop now," she pointed.

Scoop strutted boldly toward Sonya and her friends like he owned the neighborhood. "How's my girl?" he asked, moving close into Sonya's face. He puckered his lips, expecting a kiss.

Sonya looked at Brittany, then at Damo. "What you lookin' at them for?" he asked. "And who is this dude anyway?" The look on his face hardened. He took two steps forward in Damo's direction.

"This is my good friend Damo," Sonya announced nervously.

Damo held out his hand waiting for a pound from Scoop. "What's up, dawg?" Damo said trying to be hip.

"Dawg? Mannnnnnn, I'on know you. And I'm not your dawg. Besides, I'on want another dude hangin' 'round my girl. You feel me?" he asked directing his comment toward Sonya.

Damo frowned, took a step back with his long slender legs, and headed out of the complex. "I'm out."

Brittany stood with her arms folded. "I know you didn't just let that happen. Damo has been your friend forever and you gon' let this nobody talk trash to him?" Brittany waited for Sonya to answer. "You hear me?"

"She don't, but I do," Scoop responded, invading Brittany's space. He stood two inches from her face, and made sure he put fear in his voice as he spoke. "Sonya is my girl," he shouted. "I tell her what to do. Not you! You feel me?"

Brittany couldn't concentrate on Scoop's comment, because the guy headed her way scared the mess of out of her. He'd been watching the whole conversation for a while and was obviously coming over as back-up for Scoop. His dreads swung back and forth like baby snakes, and scared Brittany even more than Scoop did. "I'm leaving Sonya," she uttered.

"Don't come back either," Scoop yelled, "unless you got a death wish."

"Don't talk to my friend like that!" Sonya shouted, as she watched Brittany back away with quick strides.

Instantly, Scoop grabbed Sonya by the neck tightly, and backed her up against a nearby car. "Don't ever disrespect me like that. You feel me?"

Sonya shook her head, just as her body trembled deep inside. Water filled her eyes, but she refused to cry. The onlookers laughed and acted as if she should've known better. Scoop eventually loosened the grip on her neck. "Now, that's my girl," he said. "Give me a kiss."

Everyone watched to see if Sonya would kiss him, or take off running. She turned slightly, realizing both Brittany and Damo were completely out of sight. She leaned in slowly and kissed Scoop directly on the lips. He felt soooooooo good. For her, his kiss felt secure, it felt pleasant, something she'd never experienced before. It didn't matter that she had a reddish fingerprint mark around her neck. It was official, she was hooked. Scoop held his arm below her waist and introduced her to the boys in the hood as his new girl.

Everyone seemed to be pretty cool except for the one bald-headed guy who shouted, "Ask him what happened to his last girlfriend."

Scoop placed his hands over both of Sonya's ears as he and his boys fell out laughing. "You real funny, dawg," he joked.

━━━━━━━━━

Sonya spent the next hour having the time of her life. Strangely, she enjoyed Scoop's company in the midst of such a dysfunctional environment. They were clearly from different worlds. Sonya grew up in a house with supervision, while Scoop revealed his parents left him with a family friend at the age of twelve. Now at seventeen, he was pretty much on his own, without any rules or parenting.

The couple had been cuddled together on the footstep of a Chinese restaurant just talking. Finally, Scoop figured he'd ask Sonya if she was hungry.

"I guess a little food would be good. My aunt is making dinner I'm sure."

Sonya looked at her watch getting a sudden reality check. It was already close to five 'o'clock, and her aunt and uncle would be getting home soon.

"What you having?" Scoop asked, standing in front of the bullet proof glass.

"Chicken wings will be fine."

"Ay…give my girl three chicken wings and frics. She want mumbo sauce,"
he shouted to the robotic looking, Asian cashier.

"Oh, no mumbo sauce," Sonya called out.

"Yeah...give it to her," Scoop announced firmly. "You my girl. You eat what I tell you to eat."

Sonya smiled, although she felt a bit embarrassed. Why did Scoop wanna tell her what to eat? she wondered.

Scoop grabbed her hand and pulled her slightly behind him, headed to a table near the back of the carry-out. "So, your old boyfriend never took you out for food before, huh?"

"…Not exactly."

"What's not exactly mean. Yes or no?"

"Well, I've never had a boyfriend before."

Scoop burst into laughter. His body fell all over the table like he couldn't stop. For Sonya, she was just happy to see him smiling, and not with that hard look he normally wore on his face.

"That's funny, huh," Sonya finally asked.

"No doubt. I guess I should be proud to be your first?"

"Yep."

"I never dated a girl with braces before."

"Is that good or bad," Sonya asked, waiting for approval.

"That's hot," Scoop revealed, sticking a straw in Sonya's peach soda. "You're hot," he added, "the braces, the looks, and even your hair. I like it out and long like it is now, not in that ponytail you wear all the time."

Sonya had a weird look on her face. But she agreed with a head nod.

"Look, I gotta keep it real. It's something I need you to know. Where I'm from, girls and guys aren't just buddies. So you and that Damo dude are finished. You hear me?"

Sonya frowned. "Damo has been my friend since the fourth grade. We're just friends, that's it."

"It's either me, or him."

Scoop's tone frightened Sonya. Luckily, their number was called and Scoop rose from the seat to pick up the food. As he walked away, Sonya reconfigured her plastic smile. She wanted Scoop badly as a boyfriend, but his raging ways troubled her.

"Did you miss me," he joked, as he slid back into the booth.

"Sure did." Sonya managed to give up a half of a smile.

Instantly, Scoop devoured his wings and mumbo sauce as if he hadn't eaten all week. Sonya watched him closely wondering where he'd learned his table manners. Still in all, he was her man, so commenting on his habits wasn't gonna happen. Instead, Sonya politely ate her food slowly, and ladylike, just as Uncle Joe had taught her.

"So are you going to college?" Sonya asked.

Scoop laughed. "Does a snake have four legs?" He

laughed again then downed a Pepsi cola like he hadn't had anything to drink in ages.

"I'm serious, Scoop. I'm probably gonna go to Spellman in Atlanta if I get accepted. It would be great if you could be there too."

"We'll see," he said reluctantly. "I've got other things to take care of."

"Well for me, it's important. My mother attended Spellman, so I want to follow in her footsteps.

Scoop just nodded and for the first time listened to Sonya spill her guts about her real mother and father. Time passed, and before Sonya knew it, the street lights had come on in Shephard's Terrance. Several police cars seemed to circle the area where Scoop and Sonya walked. Her eyes widened at the drunken men who held their hands out asking her for money. Scoop chuckled while Sonya cringed.

"I think I better get home," she said, glancing at her watch. "It's almost eight. My curfew is soon," she lied.

"Oh…what time you gotta be in?"

"Nine. But I gotta work on this paper that's due tomorrow."

"I'ma have my boy drive you home."

"No…. that's…"

Before Sonya could object, Scoop had summoned a red-haired hyperactive boy over to whisper in his ear. Within seconds, the deal was made.

"Look here Sonya…" Scoop stood with his hands deep in his jean pockets, pushing his pants further off his hips. "I'on feel like getting no stares from your uncle tonight. Ray-Ray gonna get you home safely, and I'll holla at you tomorrow."

Sonya turned in Ray-Ray's direction. He seemed more like a clown than a killer, by the way he danced around and smiled in front of them. "I guess…" she responded hesitantly.

51

"Oh, he my man…he good. Call me when you get in the house."

Scoop leaned over to give Sonya a juicy kiss. She jerked back a bit, just so she could keep one good eye on Ray-Ray, who was now walking toward a Crown Vic with shiny rims.

Immediately, Sonya walked toward the car, hoping her ride home would be safe. Her mind raced thinking about how she was gonna make it in the house without her uncle seeing her get out of a car seen in a rap video.

"Ay…wait a second," Scoop called out. "I almost forgot…"

"Forgot what?" Sonya turned to say.

"This." Scoop unzipped his black hoodie and revealed a huge gold chain that read- SCOOP. "Here, this is for you to wear," he said proudly, pulling the chain off his neck, and placing it around hers.

Sonya felt honored, but felt words weren't necessary. She slid into the back seat, of the Crown Vic as if she were being chauffeured, holding onto the chain. Immediately, Ray-Ray blasted *Mrs. Officer*, by Lil' Wayne and sped off making a u-turn out of the lot, on two wheels. Sonya said a silent prayer hoping the ten minute car ride wouldn't turn into a deadly tragedy for her.

Before long, they'd pulled onto the block next to Sonya's street. "Right here," she yelled to Ray-Ray, who was still bobbing his head. Thankfully, he hadn't stopped moving in his seat to the beats since they left Scoop, which left no room for conversation.

"Thanks for the ride," Sonya said, hoping out onto the dark street.

"No doubt. Anything for Scoop."

Sonya started moving quickly, headed in the opposite direction of Ray-Ray's vehicle. She walked as fast as she could, hoping she could turn the corner before he turned his car around. Luckily, Ray-Ray never turned back around. He pulled off flying straight in the opposite direction.

Sonya took off running around the corner, and onto her street. The darkness had her feeling a little spooky, but she felt one hundred percent safer than she did back in Shephard's Terrace. As she walked past the neatly trimmed manicured yards, she wondered what her uncle would say. She'd already had every line ready to throw at him, if and when he asked certain questions.

Sonya stuck her key in the doorknob, nice and easy. It crept slowly, like in an old scary movie. Sonya placed her hand over her chest as she shut the door with her other hand. The moment she turned, she gasped! Uncle Joe's huge shadow lurked in the darkness. He was dressed in a gray pair of sweats and an oversized t-shirt, looking as if he'd just gotten home from the gym.

"Now just where have you been?"

"I…was…"

"No need to stutter," he shouted. "It's ten o'clock at night."

Aunt Lisa jetted past, folding her newspaper and shooting Sonya an 'I told you so look.' "Good night you two," she uttered, as if she were afraid to be in their presence.

"Oh, it's gonna be far from a good night," he uttered, moving closer toward Sonya. "Now, where you say you been?"

"At Brittany's house."

No matter how many times she'd practiced her lines in the car, it wasn't working.

"I had a project I was working on. I needed help."

Sonya figured the Brittany excuse would work. Out of all of her friends, Brittany was the friend he liked most. She always listened to his stories and precautions about life and

53

young boys, so she figured between Brittany's house and mentioning school work would be a winner.

Uncle Joe folded his arms and studied Sonya intensely. "Project, huh?"

"Yeah…a project." Sonya tried to zip her lightweight jacket up to her chin, hoping her new chain wouldn't show.

"What subject," he quickly asked.

"Science."

"About what in Science?"

"Uncle Joe…stop it!" she shouted. "I'm not a baby anymore!"

"And you're not grown either," he said, heading up the stairs. "And you know what else?"

"What?" Sonya asked, as her eyebrows crinkled with curiosity.

"You're not a good liar either. You're grounded. Two weeks, baby girl!"

═══════════════

The next morning Sonya jetted out of bed shortly after 6 a.m. She'd cried all night long, and could feel the swelling beneath her eyes. Puffiness of the eyes was something she'd gotten used to over the past year. But Sonya had truly reached her boiling point with her uncle.

Taking two stairs at a time, she ran down the steps and into the kitchen to call Brittany, since her uncle had graciously taken her phone from her room the night before. The whole punishment thing seemed a bit much in Sonya's eyes, but talking to Brittany was the focus for now.

The phone rang and rang while Sonya paced the floor hoping she would answer. School started at 8:30, so she was sure Brittany hadn't left home yet. Sonya's body felt weird. A sense of nervousness along with rebellion filled her spirit. After countless tries, Sonya gave up, and headed upstairs to shower and get ready for school. Fortunately for her, the house remained quiet as if her aunt and uncle were either still sleeping, or had already headed out for work.

By the time Sonya left the house, her entire disposition had changed. She'd spiral curled her hair into long tresses that touched the tip of her shoulders, and wore a fitted v-neck shirt that showed off Scoop's name piece proudly. She couldn't wait to get to school in hopes that Scoop would show up at least by third period. Sonya had thought about him all night, hoping that her family wouldn't mess up her chances of staying his girl. She smiled at the thought.

Before long, Sonya entered the front doors of Greenbriar High, and started her search for Brittany. Immediately, heads turned as she walked the long hallway with Scoop's thick chain hanging from her neck. Whisper after whisper Sonya smiled, loving the attention.

"What's up Sonya," a bystander asked, who stared at the chain intensely. "Oh nothing. You seen Brittany?"

"Yeah…I think she went to her locker."

With that said, Sonya jetted down the hallway, up the stairs, and onto the tenth grade hallway. She could see Brittany crowded around a group of girls chatting near her locker.

"Brit," Sonya called out.

At the sound of her voice, Brittany turned away, and rolled her eyes.

Sonya didn't care. She walked directly into the circle, gave her morning shout outs, and pulled Brittany away by the arm. "I've been calling you all night and all morning. I know you saw that I called."

Brittany seemed a bit standoffish. "Yeah I know." She hunched her shoulders carelessly. "Oh, so now you got the killer's chain on, huh?"

"He's not a killer, Brittany. And that's not why we need to talk. I need you to cover for me if my uncle calls you. I told him I was with you last night."

"Sonya, you're so stupid," she giggled sarcastically. "Uncle Joe called me yesterday about seven. He knows you weren't with me."

Sonya took two steps back and brushed her back against the locker. Her jaw hung low as the shock swam through her body.

"You could've at least called to tell me."

"I'm sure you and Scoop have it all under control."

Just then, one of the girls, who Brittany had left in the huddle stepped in Sonya's direction. With her hands on her hip, and a funky attitude, she made sure Sonya didn't think she was special. "Did you know Alecia had that chain on last month. Watcha self girl…he ain't nothing special."

Sonya gritted her teeth. "Hater."

"Ha- that's funny. See how much I'm hatin' when you wearing one of his black eyes."

The sound of the bell came at the perfect moment. Mr. Johnson yelled from the top of the hallway, "Clear my hallway now. I need everyone in class!"

Brittany grabbed Sonya by the arm as everyone scattered. She pulled her girl close and looked deep into her face. "Listen Sonya, Scoop is bad news. Everyone knows it, but you. You my girl, but you changing. Don't get hurt, okay?"

"What do you mean? He's not gonna hurt me. I'm his girl," she added, watching Mr. Johnson swing his walkie talkie near his waist-side.

"Look, I don't wanna get a late slip fooling with you. Stop being so naive!" Brittany said, with a raised voice. "He's got a history of abusing females. He's beat every girlfriend he's ever had."

Sonya stood shaking her head from right to left, not

believing a word her girl had said.

"Ladies, why are you still standing here?" Mr. Johnson asked, as his tall frame towered over the girls. "Class has started. Now move it, unless you wanna meet me in my office. And you know what else…"

Mr. Johnson stopped talking mid sentence and peered down at Sonya's neck. "Craig? You are wearing the awful chain of Craig! That boy is not for you Sonya. Does your uncle know about this?"

Tears welled up in Sonya's eyes. She was tired of being badgered every where she stepped in life. Instantly, she ran off, headed toward the bathroom. Under normal circumstances, she would've gotten written up. But Mr. Johnson knew she needed a moment. He nodded in Brittany's direction, giving her permission to run behind her.

"Three minutes Brittany. That's all I'm giving you two. I'll be right here," Mr. Johnson explained, looking at his watch.

The moment Brittany entered the bathroom, she wrapped her arms around her good friend who stood sniffling in front of the mirror. "Sonya, it's okay. You just gotta think, that's all. Everywhere you go, people are gonna say the same thing about Scoop."

"But he's not all bad, He's nice to me," she announced, drying her tears with the back of her hand.

"Yeah for now. He's controlling you already. Can't you see it? Look at how he dissed Damo. I mean Damo is one of your best friends."

"He said it's nothing against him Brit. He just docsn't want his girl hanging out with other males."

"So you let him dictate who your friends are gonna be?"

"No…it's not that."

"It is," Brittany shot back strongly. "I mean you really

need to learn what true friendship is about. Oh, and family too. I mean your uncle loves you dearly and you don't even appreciate it. I wish I had a father figure in my life to protect me. But I don't'," she said sadly. "So, I gotta think at all times, and protect myself."

Sonya looked at Brittany, and for once realized she was right. She didn't say it with words, but her solemn expression showed it.

"Look, Mr. Johnson is waiting outside the door, so we gotta go, but remember this one thing. Remember Uncle Joe's story about testing a guy?"

"Yeah."

"Well, tell Scoop you've decided to remain friends with Damo and see what happens. His true colors will show. And Sonya..." she turned to say, headed out of the bathroom door. "If he ever hits you, tell everyone...your uncle, the school, me...everyone. 'Cause believe me, if he hits you once, he'll do it again."

Brittany opened to door only to be greeted by Mr. Johnson who walked both girls to class and nodded his approval to the teachers for entrance into class.

━━━━━━━━━━

Nearly a week passed, and life without seeing Scoop seemed to have Sonya in a frenzy. She'd talked to him each and every night until the wee hours of the morning, causing her to spend her days at school dragging from class to class. For her, it was clearly worth it all. Love...love...love...love-it's what she felt in her heart.

As she laid across her sister, Angel's bed, her eyes remained glassy-eyed as she continued to think about Scoop.

"I thought you were gonna help me?" Angel whined to her sister. Her small, nine- year-old frame mimicked her sister's petite physique. Together, they weighed one-hundred and seventy pounds.

Angel looked at the books sprawled across her bed, and toward her sister who remained in a daze.

"Sonya, are you okay?"

"Huh?"

"Are you okay? You don't seem the same anymore," Angel commented.

"I'm in love." She smiled. "That's all," Sonya replied, as she sat straight up and grabbed the fourth grade math book. "You're not into to boys yet, so you wouldn't understand."

"Yuck…noooooooo way."

Sonya laughed at her sister's comment and at her snagged tooth in the right corner of her mouth. She threw the pillow at her sister. "If Scoop had a little brother, you'd like him. Scoop is sooooooo cute."

"I doubt it," Angel announced in a negative tone. "Plus, if his brother acts like him, I know I wouldn't like him for sure."

Angel's facial expression changed. It was obvious someone had been talking to her about Scoop. Sonya just stared for seconds waiting for her younger sister to reveal what she knew.

"Oh…so they've talked bad about him even to you, didn't they?"

"No," Angel shot back strongly. She shook her head back and forth. "I heard Uncle Joe talking to your Vice Principal. He called and told him about some girl that Scoop beat up badly a few months ago."

"Stop right there!" Sonya shouted. "I'm tired of hearing all this negativity about my man!"

She stood up from the bed and paced the floor. Her hands straddled her exposed waist and belly, just as Angel stared at her sister's half shirt that read- LOVE ME.

"Uncle Joe knows best, Sonya! He says he talks to us, so we'll know how to survive in this world. He knows all about bad boys. He says we shouldn't be serious about a guy until after college anyway." She smiled widely, hoping her sister wasn't mad at her. "He says they come a dime a dozen." She grinned.

"Listen, I' not mad at you. You're only nine. I'm mad at our uncle. He's not gonna stop me from seeing Scoop. I get off punishment tomorrow…so watch me. We're spending my birthday weekend together, and there's nothing Uncle Joe, or anybody else can do about it!"

The ringing of the phone cut the conversation short. Angel answered, and seemed a bit uneasy as she handed Sonya the phone. "You're still on punishment she whispered. But it's Damo, so I guess it's okay."

Sonya snatched the phone. "What's up?" she said with energy.

Whatever Damo said on the other end had her interest. Luckily, the two friends had worked out their differences the day before at lunch, and had been spending time together again. For the moment, at least her mind had been taken off of Scoop.

Friday came faster than Sonya expected. The previous day she'd spent hours washing, and spiral curling her hair, trying to look like the perfect girlfriend for Scoop. Unfortunately for her, some of the curls had fallen during the night so she whipped her hair into a curly ponytail, knowing scoop would be disappointed. The big sixteen was less than twenty-four hours away, yet Sonya felt special the minute she and Damo stepped off the bus. The bell hadn't rung yet, so Damo and Sonya spent a few minutes hanging around and chatting with a few friends they didn't see much.

Sonya seemed to be in her glory wearing a trendy mini-skirt and a Be-Be glittery top. Of course Scoop's chain hung boldly outside her shirt for everyone to see- and gloat, she hoped. Unfortunately, no one stared at her chain, but at Scoop's angry look from afar.

He waited in the cut with an obsessive scowl, watching as Sonya laughed and joked with Damo and the others.

From the corner of her eye, Sonya could tell all eyes were on her. The eerie feeling had her spooked. By the time she turned, she notice people standing near her examining what was coming toward them. All of a sudden, chills draped her body.

Sonya knew something was terribly wrong, but refused to turn around. She wanted nothing to ruin her day; the day leading up to her date with Scoop. As the onlookers backed away fearfully, Sonya did the inevitable. She turned. Her face twisted into a bright reddish color. As the lump formed into her throat, Scoop grabbed her by the shoulder with force. He pulled her completely away from what was left from the crowd, and hit Sonya with an open hand! Slap!

Sonya yelled out. Mostly in fear, also in pain. "No!" she yelled squirming half way off the ground to release her-self from his embrace.

"Oh, you thought it was a game!" he shouted with au-thority.

Not wasting anytime, he grabbed hold of her curly ponytail. Fearfully quiet, Sonya waited not knowing what to expect next. From the corner of her eye she could see the students gathering around waiting for Scoop to do what they knew he did best. They'd never seen him perform out in the open, yet had heard the rumors and certainly seen the results.

"I told you not to hang out with that whimpy nigga,

Damo. Didn't I?" he taunted, still with a tight hold on her ponytail.

"Yessssssss," Sonya managed to say.

"You think cheating is okay! I hope he was worth it!"

"I-I-I –wasn't cheatttttttttttt-ing!"

He landed another forceful punch to the jaw. "Shut up!"

Scoop's wild behavior escalated when he saw Damo looking on fearfully. Slap! He hit Sonya once again followed by a forceful punch to the jaw. In an attempt to block the punches, Sonya managed to slip away from his grip. She set one foot in front of the other looking for an escape. The tears that had fallen so rapidly from her eyes kept her from seeing her way. Unfortunately, Scoop caught up to her, and his next hit sent her body helplessly into the unmanicured shrubbery. Face down into the ground, Sonya cried harder than she did the day her parents died. As the warm blood dripped from her mouth, she prayed what she heard was real. The sound of Mr. Johnson's voice headed her way seemed to be the only thing that would help her survive.

Instead, Scoop walked over for one final blow. He raised his foot high in the air as if he were about to kick an unwanted animal. Sonya covered her face in anticipation. She hollered the moment his timberland boot touched her bruised skin. Crouched in fetal position she bellowed as he kicked her multiple times in the torso.

Sonya had pretty much given up. The sound of Mr. Johnson's voice didn't even matter anymore. By the time his oversized frame made it through the crowd, Scoop had disappeared. The fearful crowd seemed entertained yet frightened, as Mr. Johnson screamed to the top of his lungs! Who did this! I wanna know, right now. Anybody!"

He waved his walkie-talkie around the broken circle trying to make mental notes of the witnesses. He knew they wouldn't come forward voluntarily, but someone would help him get to the bottom of the situation if forced.

Simultaneously, the crowd dispersed with the help of teachers as Sonya was pulled from the ground. As the blood dripped from her face, she held her head low, unable to look anyone in the eye.

"First. I've gotta get you to the infirmary young lady, then call your uncle. You're gonna need to go to a hospital!"

Sonya thought about objecting, then thought about the excruciating pain she felt. Scoop had hit her with some deadly kicks and punches, so internal bleeding or damages was possible. All Sonya could do was wonder why. Why me? She cried softly.

"Was it Craig?" Mr. Johnson blurted out as he guided Sonya by the arm to the front of the building.

"Noooooo," she muttered walking slowly.

"Yes, it was," Damo responded. He stood on the side entrance door with his arms folded confidently. "I"ll tell the police, her uncle, or whoever I have to tell."

"Wait for me in front of the nurses' office," Mr. Johnson ordered. "Let her lean on you, and don't let her try to stand on her own," he told Damo.

Sonya had the look that said, "No you didn't!"

Luckily, Damo didn't care, nor did he back down. Sonya was a true fried, a friend that had been beaten in broad daylight. He knew the ramifications of abuse. He too had been abused at one point in his life. An old boyfriend of his mother's had beat them both far too many times for him to remember. But for Sonya, she needed to know the first hit would not be the last if she didn't stop Scoop now.

Inside the school, Sonya lay on the bed in the nurse's office with hundreds of thoughts flooding her mind. She wondered what sent Scoop over the edge. What would make him put his hands on her so violently? His girl? She cried once again. "I thought I was his girl," she cried out softly. "Didn't that mean anything?"

Although her cries seemed as painful as the actual bruises, the baritone sound of Uncle Joe's voice outside the door changed her entire demeanor. She sat up straight on the bed, trying to wipe away her tears. She needed to be strong, hoping to act as if things weren't as bad as they seemed. What would she say? How would she face him? Would she tell him the truth when he wanted to know the details? And most importantly, would he go after Scoop?'

All of a sudden the curtain was snatched back with a heavy hand. Uncle Joe and Mr. Johnson stood side by side with threatening looks on their faces. Joe stared with glossy eyes at his oldest niece in a terrible situation. His heart wrung with hurt, and anger filled him rapidly. "A baby, she's just a baby," he moaned to Mr. Johnson. What kinda thug is this guy," he shouted.

"Let's keep her calm," the school nurse bellowed. "She needs to get to the emergency room for x-rays."

Uncle Joe nodded, and helped Sonya from the bed. She never looked him in the eye, but felt safe as she walked up under him holding him by the waist.

"I'll be in touch," Joe said to Mr. Johnson.

"Remember what I said," Mr. Johnson called out. "Don't do anything stupid. I'm gonna have him expelled. We'll get the cops involved too. I think that's enough."

"We'll see about that," he smirked, headed out the door.

═══════════════

A day and a half had gone by without much motion from Sonya. She'd managed to allow her birthday to slip by without even emerging from her room. Sixteen, sickly, and stupid, she thought to herself. What a life!

Each and every time her aunt or uncle would pass her room, she'd make sure her eyes remained lowered. Although embarrassed, she felt protected under her uncle's roof. After the way Scoop acted up she wasn't sure if he was gonna try to come to the house unannounced. He'd called a few times in a twenty-four hour period, yet remained persistent. Ashley told Sonya that she'd overheard Uncle Joe telling Scoop if he ever came near her again, he was gonna be six feet under!"

Sonya sat solemnly near the edge of the bed thinking about how Uncle Joe made her go to the police station immediately after they left the hospital. It was crucial that she filed charges on Scoop immediately after the incident. Sonya placed her head into her palms thinking about how she had to pose so the officer's could take pictures of the bruises for evidence. She begged her uncle not to have him locked up. To no avail, he wasn't going for it. The officer's located a picture of Scoop from a previous incident and placed a warrant out for his arrest.

Sonya wanted to cry once again, but felt someone's presence near her door. She turned just in time to see her uncle entering her room. She allowed a slight smile to slip from the side of her mouth.

"Feeling okay?" he asked.

Sonya nodded.

"Can I sit down?"

"Of course." Sonya slid to the left giving her uncle some space.

"I see you always hold the side of your jaw. Is everything healing okay, or should we go back to the doctor again."

"I'm fine. My braces still hurt every now and then, but I'll be okay. The nurse told me to expect that."

"Look, this situation is hard on everyone around here. I-I-I just want you to know that we love you... and I only want the best for you," he blurted out.

"I know."

"What you don't know is that I saw something bad in Scoop's eye the day I met him. I've seen so many young thugs like him before. I just wanted to protect you." He grabbed her hand to console her. "I know you think I'm hard on you…but this is why?"

Tears welled up in Sonya's eyes. She felt three feet tall while her uncle professed what he saw in her wanna-be boyfriend. The same guy she thought was so great. Yet still in all, Sonya still had a strong desire to give Scoop another chance. "I don't know why….but…but I still love him," she confessed.

"What the heck!" Uncle Joe rose from the bed in a fury. His knuckles cracked as he banged one fist into the other.

"Just hear me out. I'm not saying I'll see him again…"

Uncle Joe interrupted, "I know good darn well you won't! You have a court date where you will testify against him and tell the judge what he did to you!"

"See, I can't talk to you!"

"No. You can't when it sounds stupid. Abuse is serious. Once someone abuses you, nine times out of ten they will do it again. There's a reason why domestic violence has increased over the last few years in high school students."

"And why is that?" Sonya asked with sarcasm.

"Oh, don't get cute. I may not know why, but I watch the news and read the paper. Young girls out here lack self esteem when they allow these little thugs to physically abuse them. I'm just not sure how you fell into that category. I raised you better than that," he huffed.

"I didn't just let him. He overpowered me. Besides, how was I supposed to know he was gonna put his hands on me?"

"Oh, he didn't just put his hands on you. That lil' sucka whipped your tail. I'm just waiting for the chance to show him something!"

Sonya looked carefully at the strange look her uncle wore on his tiring face. It seemed a bit deranged, yet concerned. "Auntie told you not to do anything crazy. Forget about it. It's over," Sonya added.

"Yeah…just remember your words. It's over."

" I knowwwwwwww," Sonya responded in an irritated tone.

"I got a question. Didn't you hear all the stories about this guy with other girls? Or didn't he portray any signs of excessive control?"

Sonya shrugged her shoulders. She thought about Scoops attempt to tell her what to eat, how to wear her hair, and who she could be friends with. But it was clear she didn't want to talk about it with her uncle.

"Well, if I can help it, you'll never have to see his face again. We got Damo, Brittany, and Mr. Johnson who will all testify to what they saw and serve as character witnesses. And we all know what his character is like."

Joe leaned in to kiss his battered niece on the cheek. Something he hadn't done in years. As he raised his body away from Sonya's, he allowed his fingers to softly rub the side of her face to caress the largest bruise on the left side of her cheek.

"Thanks Uncle Joe for everything. I mean it," she said as he left the room.

Days passed, and before long Sonya's bruises had started to heal. She finally felt comfortable enough to be seen in public. She rushed down the stairs and grabbed her Juicy sweat-jacket off the railing near the bottom of the steps. Sonya reached for the door until the ringing of the phone caught her off guard.

"Hello," she said cheerfully.

Her facial expression changed instantly. It couldn't have happened at a worse time. His voice, his spirit…it all freaked her out.

"Why are you calling me Scoop?"

"'Cause you my girl. Aren't you?"

"Not anymore. And if my uncle was here, he'd have some words for you."

"Oh…where he at? Tell him to get with me," he bragged.

"Look, I'm on my way out."

"Let's meet up so we can talk. You seem to be home alone, right."

"Yeah." She hesitated thinking about what she'd just said. She glanced at the old fashioned wooden clock on the wall. Uncle Joe would be home soon, so having Scoop come by to talk was a no-no. Besides, there was nothing to talk about. The weird part about it all was that Sonya enjoyed hearing his voice. "On second thought Scoop, I gotta go."

"Wait," he shouted. "You're not really gonna testify against me, are you?"

Silence infiltrated the phone line.

"Uhhhhhhhhhh….I guess…"

"Sonya, listen. I'm almost to your house. I'll be there in two minutes."

Sonya's jaw dropped and her mouth was left wide open.

It took nearly ten minutes for her to snap from the daze and realize she either needed to call her uncle or get out of the house. With a rapid pace, she reached for the front door, only to find Scoop standing there with a fake smile on his face and his hands in his pocket.

"We oughta make up Sonya. I'm sorry."

Scoop sounded very apologetic and sincere. He held his arms open wide. Sonya wanted so badly to enter his embrace, but knew it was the wrong thing to do.

"So, you just gon' leave a brotha standing here on the porch?"

"Scoop, you hurt me!" she shouted.

"You disrespected me!" he yelled back.

"How? And does that mean I deserved this!" She pointed toward the only visible bruise remaining on her face.

"You gotta learn to listen," he shouted. "If you hadn't been hanging around that dude Damo, none of this woulda happened."

Scoop realized his voice level had gotten out of hand. He quickly calmed himself down. "Sonya just do as I say, and we'll be okay."

"No! I am going to be around Damo. He's my friend. Besides, you're not my boyfriend."

Whop! Sonya was hit directly in the face. She couldn't believe this was happening again. Flashbacks of Uncle Joe's words flashed through her mind. *Once someone abuses you, they will do it again.*

Sonya had given up. Scoop had access to her house, and had stepped inside. The more she backed away, the angrier he became. Before long, Sonya had become dizzy. As thoughts flooded her mind, Scoops tall frame became blurry. Out of the blue, Sonya blacked out.

Twelve hours later, Sonya sat in her living room surrounded by family and friends listening to how Uncle Joe came home and beat the living crap out of Scoop. They rejoiced in how blessed Sonya was to have a guard dog like Joe who showed up shortly after she blacked out.

"I'm so glad Scoop came on your property," Brittany uttered. "Now we know the breaking and entering charges will stick."

"Shoot, the assault charges will stick too," Damo chimed in. "We got him for sure." He smiled and looked at Sonya who sat confidently near her uncle.

"I'm sorry I never saw what you guys saw," Sonya revealed. "I was dumb and thought I was in love. But now I know that wasn't true love. He was crazy all along and I just didn't want to accept it. For a minute, I really believed he was sorry for what he'd done to me."

"It's okay, baby girl. We all make mistakes. Just know that a boy, man, male, or anybody other than your father, or male provider should not put his hands on you. And even then, it should be appropriate punishment, not abuse."

"Got it," Sonya responded quickly.

For the first time in days she wore a bright smile. She'd been assured by the police that Scoop would be locked up until the court date, and not released quickly like before. He would have to go before a judge on charges of breaking and entering and assault and battery. This time, Sonya didn't feel any hesitation about testifying. It was something that had to be done.

"You still love him?" Uncle Joe asked curiously.

"No way!" Sonya shouted. "Any boy who would want to hurt me doesn't love me, right?" She grinned. "See, I told you I'm listening to your life lessons."

Sonya seemed to have thrown away any love in her heart for Scoop. With her friends by her side she was full of self esteem. Her requirements for a boyfriend had changed drastically. Education was #1 and 2- they had to be completely checked out by Uncle Joe.

"Damo, what's your social security number boy. I gotta get you checked out too," Uncle Joe asked in an animated voice.

The entire room erupted into laughter after Uncle Joe's comment. Sonya smiled. She loved her family and vowed to make smarter decisions in life, especially when it came to choosing a boyfriend.

Teenage Bluez

THE N-WORD

by Marketa Salley

Seven thirty rolled around quickly just as Brandon was about to play his last game at Spingarn High School. Sitting in the locker room, he tried to get his mind in game mode.

"Hey B…this it man," his teammate yelled. "Let's go get um."

Brandon walked slowly down the hall toward the court. When he emerged the crowd went crazy.

"Brandon, Brandon, Brandon," the crowd chanted onc after another. Hearing the crowd recite his name made him feel a little better, but seeing his mother along with his friends Ray-Ray and T-Bone, put a big smile on his face. This was the first time his mother was able to attend a game since she accepted her new job. The fact that she was sitting courtside made the moment even more special.

As the guys warmed up, Brandon looked around the gym.

"Who you lookin' for?" Brandon's coach asked.

"I was lookin' to see if there are any scouts here tonight."

"You know doggone well ain't no scouts crazy enough to come up in here. It's a war zone. It's much safer for them to just watch you on tapes," his coach said.

Brandon laughed but it wasn't a laughing matter. All his life, he used to tell himself that he was going to go to the best college and get drafted by the NBA. Now he wasn't sure, and all because most of the scouts from the big schools were slightly afraid to come to his school, or any inner city school to watch him play. Every time a scout made a commitment to see him play, a fight would break out before the first quarter ended.

Sure enough, thirty minutes into the game a fight broke out. This time an unexpected culprit was involved, his friend Dashawn. Brandon didn't even know Dashawn had showed up to the game, because he wasn't sitting with his other friends. He'd obviously walked into the gym to watch Brandon play when a guy from a rival neighborhood went over and confronted Dashawn about trying to take his girlfriend out. Their verbal confrontation ended up getting physical.

Dashawn hung in there with the guy even though he was much taller and bigger than he was. When another guy jumped on Dashawn, an all out brawl started between the two rival neighborhoods, including T-Bone and Ray-Ray. The guys were jumping out of the bleachers and swinging on anyone who wasn't from their hood, and the girls were pulling weaves, kicking, and scratching. They were so out of control teachers and parents who were trying to break the fights up just couldn't contain them. To top it off, in the midst of all the commotion someone pulled the fire alarm causing innocent bystanders to get trampled when everyone started scrambling to get out of there.

After the police broke up the fights they cleared the gym. Janae quickly ran to the locker room, and waited for Brandon to get dressed. When he finally showed his face, Janae spoke loudly, "We need to go!"

"Ma, I was going wit my man's and dem to see the TCB band," Brandon whined.

"Oh no! You're going home. Did you see what just happened out there?" Janae asked, grabbing Brandon by the arm.

Brandon looked around. "Ma, you gotta stop treatin' me like a baby," he whispered. "That could've happened anywhere, and in any state."

Janae sighed deeply. She wanted to protect Brandon from all the dangers of their neighborhood like the gambling, drugs, and gun violence. That's why she'd worked so hard to earn the newest promotion at her job so she could move them away. She was finally able to accomplish her dream of giving her son a better life, so she figured she'd let him hang out one last time with his friends before they moved to Virginia the following month.

"Listen, I'm gonna let you go out with your friends, but make good choices. There's a rumor going on around here that all that mess tonight was because of Dashawn."

"Not true, Ma," Brandon lied.

Brandon and his friends Dashawn, T-Bone, and Ray Ray had known each other just about their whole lives, so they always covered for one another. They were all the same age and would eat over each other's houses regularly. If you messed with one, you had to take them all on.

Although they all lived in the same rough neighborhood, Brandon was the only one who had a real chance of making it big, because of his skills on the basketball court. Dashawn was what you would call a bun...a very handsome guy. He was 5'6", muscular, with light brown eyes, and had long braids. The girls loved him while all the guys hated him.

Brandon noticed his mother staring at him from the corner of his eye. "What's up? You're embarrassing me," he said scanning the area to see who was watching them.

"I know you think I'm a little overprotective."

"A little? You're like a warden," he said giggling.

"Do you wanna go out?"

"I'm just playin', Ma."

Janae grabbed his hand. "I'm overprotective, because I don't want *you* to end up like *your* father."

Janae went on to explain to Brandon how his father was a working man, but his friends were in the streets.

"I've never told you the whole story, but you're sixteen now, and old enough to know." A tear fell from her eye. "Your father was on his way home from work when his friend asked him to take a ride with him. They were sitting at a light when a guy drove up and just started shooting at them."

"Why did the guy shoot at them?"

"He wasn't shooting at your father. He was trying to shoot his friend, because he owed him money." Janae wiped away the tears that were streaming down her face. "In other words watch the company you keep. You understand?"

"Yeah, Ma, I understand," Brandon said, hugging her tightly. He kissed her then ran over to T-Bone, Ray-Ray, and Dashawn, who were all checking their watches.

When Brandon and his friends arrived at the recreation center, the line was wrapped around the building. That didn't surprise them though, because of the popularity of the TCB band and their new style of Go-Go music.

Go-Go is a subgenre of funk that originated in the Washington D.C. area during the mid- to late-1970s. A handful of bands contributed to the early evolution of the genre, but singer-guitarist Chuck Brown is credited with having developed most of the hallmarks of the style. While Go-Go's international profile was on the rise in the 1980s, go-go clubs in D.C. were acquiring an unfortunate reputation for violence....yet Brandon and his crew wanted to be a part of it. Brandon knew his mom didn't like him attending events like that, but he figured one night wouldn't hurt.

The boys walked up to the front of the line.

"Main man, let us in!" Dashawn yelled.

The bouncer looked past Dashawn, and straight at Brandon. "Ain't you that ball player from Spingarn?" he asked.

"Yeah, that's me," Brandon said, beaming. "You think you can let me and my boys in?"

"Come on in," the bouncer said. "Just remember me when you make it big."

"I will," Brandon replied, as he walked past the bouncer proudly.

Once the boys were inside they found a spot and posted up against the wall. They watched as girl after girl walked by, signaling each other when they saw someone they liked. T-Bone saw a lot of girls he liked, the only probably was they didn't like him back. Out of the four of them, he was the least attractive. He was short, skinny, and had light patches on his dark skin. His mother never took him to the dentist when he was a kid so his teeth were stained, crooked and full of cavities. Nevertheless, his boys loved him.

Brandon just shook his head, "Is that all y'all niggas think about?"

"Yep. Don't you?" T-Bone asked jokingly, showing every tooth in his mouth, even the space where one was missing.

"A girl gotta be a straight dime piece in order to get me off my game," Brandon announced.

While the TCB band was on stage setting up, the boys mingled with some of the other guys from their neighborhood. Minutes later, Polo the leader of the band checked his mic. "One, two…one, two." Then the rest of the band started warming up.

The band started going down their playlist, hitting some of their older songs like *I Need a Girl* and *London Bridge*. When they played *Wipe Me Down* everyone started repping their hoods. The boys were having fun. Brandon was especially having fun, because Polo gave him a special shout out.

"Hey yo…I'm the man around here son," Brandon said, popping his collar.

Everything was alright until the guy Dashawn had gotten into the fight with at the game saw him dancing with his girlfriend. The guy wasted no time stepping to Dashawn.

"Nigga what's up? Why you all up on my girl?" the guy asked.

Dashawn moved even closer. "I ain't all up on your girl. Your girl's all up on me."

"So what, you tryin' to see me again?" the guy asked.

"It's whatever nigga."

Brandon, T-Bone, and Ray-Ray tried to intervene, but Dashawn was too quick with his hands. He landed a right hook on the guy's chin.

Next thing you knew, it was total mayhem. After several minutes of fist flying mid-air, and people being knocked to the ground, the bouncers finally got the brawl under control. They threw Dashawn, the guy he was fighting, and anyone else they suspected of causing the disturbance out of the center first.

Polo, grabbed the mic, "Hey, yo…since ya'll don't know how to act, we shuttin' it down." He then signaled for his band to pack it up.

After being thrown out of the recreation center, Brandon, Ray-Ray, T-Bone, and Dashawn headed to the subway station.

"Nigga, you got to calm down," Ray-Ray said to Dashawn. "You messin' it up for all of us."

"Shut up nigga! It ain't like we can't go back next week."

"Y'all can go back but my mom's sure ain't gonna let me go back," Brandon said, walking with his head hung down.

"Oh, I forgot you a momma's boy," Dashawn teased, while playing with his braids.

"Whatever nigga! You always jonin' on somebody! Besides, you know I'm moving in a few weeks."

After that comment, the boys walked to the station in silence, then talked in moderation during the ride. But as soon as they got to the Benning Road station near their neighborhood they were back to normal.

"TCB ripped it tonight with that slow bounce beat joint," Brandon said, checking their surroundings as they exited the train station.

"I know Son," Ray-Ray replied. "The shorties were bouncin' hard when they hit that joint," he said.

"I know nigga, and I was bouncin' right along with them," T-Bone said dancing in the middle of the street.

"Ya'll niggas stupid," Brandon managed to say in between laughs.

The boys were almost home when out of nowhere, the guy Dashawn had fought ran up on them. Wearing all black, the guy pointed his gun directly at Dashawn's chest.

"What ya'll lil niggas got to say now! Huh!" he smirked. "I told ya'll I would see you again!" the guy yelled as his hand shook.

The boys stood still and never made a sound.

"Shorty, look it ain't gotta go down like this," Ray-Ray said trying to calm the guy down.

Brandon looked out the corner of his eye and saw a group of kids walking down the street towards them. He hoped that they would notice what was going on and call the police. Dashawn, the hothead of the group, had a plan of his own.

"Nigga…you ain't gonna do nothin' with that gun, cuz if you were you would've done it by now," Dashawn said, before he swung on the guy hitting him hard enough to knock him to the ground.

Once the guy was down, Dashawn gave him a few hard kicks as T-Bone, Ray-Ray, and Brandon took off running. They hadn't even run fifty yards when they heard several loud popping sounds. Just as Brandon was about to duck behind a car, he heard Dashawn faintly yell his name. Brandon turned around first, only to see Dashawn falling forward, as his assailant ran down the street. It was as if everything moved in slow motion.

When Brandon and T-Bone saw Dashawn's body hit the ground, they ran to his aid.

"Ray-Ray, call for help!" T-Bone yelled, as he tried to turn Dashawn over onto his back.

"Don't move him!" Brandon screamed.

Ray-Ray, the only one with a cell phone dialed 911.

"911, can you hold please?" the male operator asked.

"Naw…nigga I can't hold! We need an ambulance! My man just got hit!"

"What did he get hit by?"

"He got shot! Why you askin' all these stupid questions just get somebody here."

"What is your location sir?"

Ray-Ray told the operator they were on the corner of B Street and Benning Road. Before the operator could say anything else he hung up. By this time, people were crowding around, many of them from their neighborhood.

Brandon, T-Bone, and Ray-Ray kneeled beside their friend and tried to keep him calm. They all took turns telling him that he had to hold on, as they all heard sirens in the background. Within minutes, the paramedics and the police were on the scene. They jumped out of their vehicles and advised the bystanders to back up.

After taking Dashawn's vital signs and hooking him up to an IV, the paramedics wheeled Dashawn away on a stretcher. Brandon walked over and asked which hospital they were taking him too.

"George Washington," the medic said, brushing past him.

The boys quickly asked around for a ride. Finally a police officer told them he would take them. Just as they were about to go, Brandon noticed that the ambulance hadn't moved.

"Yo, why they ain't left yet?" Brandon asked.

"Yeah…what's goin' on?" Ray-Ray asked the officer.

When the officer saw that the ambulance wasn't in a hurry to leave, he knew what it meant. He walked over to the ambulance and knocked on the door. When the medic opened the door, he shook his head. The officer turned and walked back to the boys.

"What's up man?" T-Bone asked the officer. "What's takin' them so long to leave?"

The officer took a deep breath before he broke the news to the boys that Deshawn had died. Shocked and grief-stricken, the boys immediately broke down.

Three Weeks Later

Brandon sat on his bed, reflecting on the tragic night he lost his friend Dashawn.

"Brandon! Brandon are you finished yet?" his mother Janae yelled from her bedroom.

Brandon took a deep breath then answered, "Yeah…I guess."

His mother stuck her head in his doorway. "Boy, I guess is not the answer I was looking for. Try yes, or no."

"Yes, Ma, I'm done."

"Thank you. I have to put a few more things in the car so I'll meet you downstairs."

"Ma, when are the movers coming to get the rest of the stuff?"

"What movers? All we're taking are our clothes and our pictures."

"What about my bed?" Brandon asked, with his eyebrows raised.

"I told you we were starting over. We're not taking any of this stuff to Virginia. I bought all new furniture. It's already set up at the new house."

It was hard for Brandon to believe that he was leaving the apartment he spent his whole life in. Within two months flat, his mother had gotten a promotion and purchased a new home, because she feared she would lose Brandon to the streets of D.C. Brandon understood, but everything was moving a little too fast for him. Moving to an all-white neighborhood was one thing, but to do it in the middle of his 11th grade year was another.

Brandon walked over to the closet and grabbed his Spalding basketball. Spinning the ball on his fingertip, he took one last look around the room he had slept in since he was a baby. *Man, I'ma miss this place,* he thought. He threw on his North Face coat, pushed his basketball under his arm then went to meet his mother at her car. When he stepped out of their building, he was met by his boys, T-Bone and Ray-Ray.

"What's good wit you?" T-Bone asked.

"What's up nigga?" Ray-Ray added.

Brandon looked over at his mother. When he saw that she was in the car, and occupied on her cell phone, he confided in his friends that he wasn't feeling the move.

"Nigga, you crazy. If my moms could get us up out of here, I wouldn't think twice bout it. I'd be gone. To tell the truth, every since that nigga took out Dashawn man, I just ain't felt safe round here," T-Bone said.

"Bone, I'm with you man." Ray-Ray took a seat on the stoop in front of Brandon's building. "B, ain't nothin' here man. Every night we gotta duck down when we hear gun-shots. We leave for school in the morning, but with no guar-antee we gonna make it back home. Think about it. You know those rich prep schools have a lot of scouts at their games."

"True," Brandon replied. He let out a deep sigh. "I guess it will be a'ight."

Janae blew the horn. "Brandon we have to go baby. The man installing the home theatre is waiting on me."

Ray-Ray's eyes almost popped out of his head. "B, y'all gonna have a theatre in ya'll crib?"

"Yeah, so as soon as my moms says it's okay, I want y'all to come over and spend the weekend."

"That's what's up nigga. Just hit us up," Ray-Ray said, standing up off the stoop. The guys gave each other one last group hug then Brandon got in the car.

"You okay Brandon?" Janae asked, peeping from the window. She wanted to get one last look at Ray-Ray and T-Bone.

When Brandon finally replied, "Yes," she slowly drove away.

═══════════════

As soon as Janae and Brandon drove through the gate of their new neighborhood in Fairfax, Virginia he was amazed at how different it was from their neighborhood in Northeast.

There were no dirty needles on the ground, it was quiet, the yards were neatly manicured, and almost every house had a luxury car parked outside of it.

"Well here it is," Janae said proudly.

Brandon's eyes were glued to the massive home before him. He couldn't even speak. Besides seeing pictures of it, this was the first time he had seen the new house in person. Every time Janae would come over to do repairs, or to inspect it with the realtor, Brandon was always doing something else.

"Ma, this house is huge."

"I know. Wait until you see the inside."

Janae led Brandon inside. They walked into the family room and were immediately greeted by a woman who appeared to be in her late fifties. She was dark skinned, medium height, and a little on the heavy side.

"Welcome young man," the woman greeted.

"Brandon, this is Ms. Odell our housekeeper," Janae revealed.

Brandon was confused. "Housekeeper? We have a housekeeper?"

Janae couldn't help but laugh at her son. She knew their new lifestyle was going to take some time to get used too. After all, they had lived in a neighborhood that was less than desirable, and before she graduated from college and received her new promotion, she could barely make ends meet.

"Brandon, why don't you let me show you the rest of the house," Ms. Odell announced.

"Alright, let's do it."

"Okay, let's start in the kitchen."

While Brandon and Ms. Odell took a tour of the house, Janae started to unpack the items from her car. While she was outside, she noticed her neighbors peeking from their windows. Janae had to make several trips to her car, so with each

84

trip, she became more uneasy. One neighbor kept opening and shutting her blinds every time Janae would look in her direction. Janae just shook her head. *Yep, I'm black and I'm here to stay*, she boasted to herself.

After she brought the last box in, she locked the door and set the alarm. A few minutes later, there was a knock at the door. *Who could that be?* She looked through the side glass and saw a beautiful, blond white woman and a teenager around Brandon's age. *Oh, I know she ain't about to start no mess with me. I might be out of the hood, but the hood is still in me.* She opened the door ready for a fight.

"Yes, can I help you," Janae said, with a little sass in her voice.

"Hello, my name is Emily Donalds and this is my son Todd. We live next door, and we just wanted to welcome you to the neighborhood."

Janae felt really bad. Here she was ready for a show-down and the woman and her son were just trying to be friendly.

"Hi, Emily, my name is Janae. Why don't you two come in?" As they walked through the hallway, Janae told them she was sorry about the mess. Once in the living room, they all took a seat.

Meanwhile, Brandon walked around shouting out, "Oohs and ahhs," as he looked at the over-sized rooms. The first place Ms. Odell took him was to the theatre room, even though it was still under construction.

"Wow," he said, testing out one of the theatre seats. "It's just like being at the movies."

"I know isn't it great? Let's check out the other rooms."

She led him down the hallway to his bedroom, which was half the size of his old apartment.

"Oh my God! This is my room?"

"Yes sir, it is."

Brandon sat down on his bed. "I've never felt a bed this soft before in my life."

Ms. Odell agreed. Her room was right across from his. Janae's was at the other end of the hallway. They continued to the gourmet kitchen then to the recreation room. It wasn't until she showed him the basketball court out back that Janae had built for him that he was actually speechless. Basketball was his life and he had big dreams of going to the NBA when he finished college.

Once the tour of the house was complete the two headed back to the family room.

"Oh sweetheart, I'm glad you're here. This is Emily Donalds and her son Todd. Emily and Todd, this is my son Brandon."

Brandon extended his hand to greet them both. "Nice to meet you."

"Nice to meet you Brandon. Your mother tells me you're a basketball star. So is Todd. He won MVP last year."

"What position do you play?" Brandon asked.

"I'm a guard. What about you? No, let me guess. Post right," Todd replied.

"True...true. I play post."

"How old are you?" Todd asked, taking notice of Brandon's six seven height.

"I'm sixteen."

"Me too," Todd added.

"Maybe we can shoot some hoops one day. I have a basketball court out back."

"I know I watched them build it. We live next door."

"Cool."

Emily hated to interrupt the two since they seemed to be hitting it off, but she needed to get home to make some phone calls.

"Well, Janae it was so nice to meet you and Brandon. Maybe we can all have dinner together one night."

Janae told her that they would be nice, as she escorted them to the front door. After they said their goodbyes, she locked the door and set the alarm.

━━━━━━━━━━

Later that night, Janae and Brandon sat down to the dinner table for their first meal in their new home. Ms. Odell had really out done herself. She made fried chicken, macaroni and cheese, cabbage, and home-made cornbread.

"Man, are we gonna have food likc 'dis every night," Brandon asked, licking his fingers.

"Brandon, what did I tell you about talking like that?" Janae asked, with a serious face. "Speak proper English, like I taught you. I see every now and then you slip up with that crazy talk."

"Sorry."

Ms. Odell smiled. "Yes sir… you are. The food will be great."

"Well, I can see right now that I'm going to be gaining a lot of weight around here."

"Don't worry, with all the running you do at practice, I think you'll be just fine. Just fine," Ms. Odell said, giving him another helping of Mac and Cheese.

Ms. Odell was from the old school. She believed kids should always havc good home cooked meals instead of fast food. She was a widower and never had kids of her own, so she had already taken a liking to Brandon. Janae was just as happy as Brandon was to have Ms. Odell around. With her hectic schedule, she knew cooking, and cleaning was going to be tough. So, after meeting Ms.Odell through a friend, she hired her after checking her references and finding out that she was a great housekeeper who had helped to raise several kids; all of them were now successful adult men and women.

When they were finished eating, Janae started to put the dishes away.

"Miss Janae, put those dishes down, that's my job. You go relax."

"Oh…okay. I'm sorry," Janae said, still not used to having Ms. Odell around.

"I understand, but you don't have to do all of this by yourself anymore. You made it, now enjoy it!"

Even though Ms. Odell had dropped out of school in the 10th grade to take care of her ailing mother she was a wise old woman who'd worked for Dr. Martin Luther King as a secretary during the Civil Rights Movement.

For some reason, she even looked wise. Her striking short, gray hair-cut made her appear distinguished, along with her extra proper tone. When she spoke she made sure to accentuate every syllable and always conversed as if she were giving a speech...only with a warm smile.

"Well, Brandon, I'm going to go my room and finish unpacking."

"Okay Ma, I'm going to go watch a little television in the family room."

"You both go take care of yourselves, I've got the housework for the night. And I'll see you both in the morning."

Once everyone was finished, they all retired to their rooms for the night.

The next morning, Brandon got up early and unpacked his belongings. He was starting school the next day and didn't want to have to dig through boxes to find something to wear. Once he finished, he headed downstairs. As soon as his foot hit the last step, a delightful smell coming from the kitchen, infiltrated his nostrils.

"Good Morning Brandon. Breakfast is almost ready. Is your mother awake?" Ms. Odell smiled.

"I think so." he said, sitting down at the table.

Janae emerged in her lavender bathrobe and slippers. "Good morning everyone," she said, taking a seat.

"Good morning," Ms. Odell replied, placing a stack of pancakes on the table.

"Good morning Ma. How did you sleep?"

"Like a baby. It's so quiet around here. How about you?"

"It was a little weird not being in my old room, but it was cool. Now if I can just get through my first day at this school."

Janae could sense Brandon wasn't happy about going to a new school, but she had already put her foot down regarding that subject.

"Man, I'm blown. I can't hang wit my friends like I use to," Brandon said, slouching in his chair.

"Look, I know this has been really hard on you. Leaving your friends, moving from one neighborhood to another, and going to a new school that you're probably not going to be welcomed in with open arms, but I've worked hard to get you out of the hood. I was scared to death you would end up like Dashawn." She grabbed Brandon's hand. "Baby, I want you to have all the things I couldn't, including a decent education."

"I know you've worked hard. Sorry, I didn't mean to sound ungrateful."

"That's okay. I know you didn't. Don't worry so much. I bet it's not going to be as bad as you think."

Just as they were about to start eating, they heard a loud thump at the door.

"What was that?" Janae asked, getting up from the table.

"I don't know," Brandon replied, following his mother to the front door.

Janae opened the door. "What in the world?"

Brandon's blood was boiling as he looked up and down the street.

"I thought the sixties were gone. I guess I thought wrong," Janae said, as she picked up the black doll with the word nigga spray painted on it and a rope tied around its neck.

"My Lord, the devil is busy," Mrs. Odell responded, shaking her head.

They all went back into the house. Janae considered calling the police, but felt there was no use. They didn't see who did it, and that would be the police's first question. *If they think they're going to run me from around here, they have another thing coming to them. I've seen and been through things they couldn't even imagine so this ain't nothing,* she thought, as they walked back to the kitchen. *Besides, most people are done with racial inequalities. So, I'm not gonna let one bad apple spoil things for us.*

"Brandon, let's sit down and enjoy our breakfast cause we ain't going nowhere. They can throw a bomb up in this camp, and I still ain't moving," Janae laughed. They all had fun with Janae's comment, trying to lighten the mood.

On the outside Janae laughed, but on the inside she was fuming. She had worked hard all her life and all she wanted to do now was to enjoy life. She was beginning to wonder if that was even possible. Like Biggie Smalls said,

"Mo Money Mo Problems."

Ms. Odell was very upset. She lived through the civil rights movement. She had been hit on, spit on, and sprayed with high pressure water from hoses during what was supposed to be peaceful protests.

Brandon on the other hand, still had the hood mentality and was ready to go out and put somebody on their back.

"Yo, I'm gonna find out who put this on our door," Brandon said, out of the blue.

Janae folded her arms. "Brandon, listen…violence never solves anything. I mean look at what happened to Dashawn. And remember…stop talking like that. You use too much slang."

Brandon sat quietly and thought about what his mother had said. She was right…violence never solves anything.

Later that day, Janae decided to go visit her good friend back in her old neighborhood. Before she left, she gave Ms. Odell the rest of the day off, so she could catch the evening Sunday service at her church. Brandon decided to stay home and research his new school's basketball stats.

"Bye baby, I'll see you later," Janae said, as she walked out the front door.

"Okay…don't be too late. You got to go to work tomorrow," Brandon replied.

"Last time I checked I was grown…so I'll be home when I get home." Janae placed her hands on her hips.

It was only thirty degrees outside, but the chill didn't stop Brandon from going outside to try his new basketball court. He threw on his coat, Retro Jordan's and grabbed his basketball before heading out. He did a warm up to loosen up then started shooting around. He'd just done his famous

crossover before shooting a three point shot from the side
when he noticed Todd peeking out of an upstairs window. He
continued to practice shots. Minutes later, Todd came out.

"Dude, what's up?"

Who is he calling, dude? Brandon thought as he kept
playing.

"Mind if I shoot around with you?" Todd asked, stepping onto the court.

"Naw, go ahead shorty," Brandon said, throwing Todd
a hard pass.

What's his deal? Todd thought. He caught the ball then
shot a three at the foul line. He repeated the same shot before
throwing the ball back to Brandon.

"So you think you got game…huh?" Brandon asked.

"I don't think. I know."

Brandon laughed. "Alright let's play a little one and
one."

"Let's do it," Todd said, bending down to tighten his
sneakers.

Brandon took the ball out first then quickly swung to
his right and laid the ball up with his left hand. Todd was in
awe of Brandon's agility. Besides their love for basketball, the
two boys were as different as they come. Brandon's height,
along with his linebacker physique made him a force to be
reckoned with. He was very dark skinned while Todd, on the
other hand, was in great need of a tan. He was also five inches
shorter and sported his blond hair spiked like a rocker.

When they were finished playing their game, Brandon
told Todd he needed to step up his game if he ever wanted to
beat him.

"You just got lucky this time," Todd said.

"Lucky, I beat you by twelve. That's not luck…that's
skill."

Tired and cold Brandon invited Todd inside for a

while.

"You want a Gatorade?" Brandon asked.

"Sure."

Brandon handed him an orange flavored Gatorade then grabbed one for himself. The two went into the family to watch 106 and Park.

"So, how do you like it out here so far?" Todd asked.

Brandon rolled his eyes. "It was alright until someone decided to throw a black doll with a rope wrapped around its neck at my door."

"Shut the front door man!"

"What? The front door isn't open."

Todd laughed. "I know…that means get out of here. You know like you're kidding me."

"Oh, and what about that dude crap?" Brandon asked, laughing.

"It's like when you called me, *shorty*. I think that sounds weird. Anyway, did you see who threw the doll at your door?"

"Naw, we were eating. I wished I had though, so I coulda shown them how we get down in the N.E."

Todd looked at Brandon confused. "The N.E.?"

"It's my old neighborhood."

"Was it nice?"

"You are really green you know that? I lived in the worst part Northeast, D.C. I had to duck bullets almost every time I stepped out of the house. There was always someone dying on my block and if you didn't know how to fight you were definitely in trouble."

"Man. I've never been in a fight in my life."

"Never?"

"Nope. How about you?"

"Shorty, I had to fight all the time. You had to show nigga's you weren't weak."

Todd stood confused for a moment when he heard Brandon use the word, *Nigga*. *I thought African-Americans didn't like that word. I thought it was degrading and needed to be buried for good.*

"Interesting," Todd said, looking at Brandon. "Well, I better go home and get ready for school tomorrow. If I find out whose behind that whole doll thing, I'll let you know," he said, drinking the last of his Gatorade.

Brandon walked Todd to the door. He was almost out the door when he suddenly turned around. "Hey, I almost forgot, basketball try-outs are tomorrow. You should try out. We could really use someone with your skills."

"I would, but I don't think they're ready for their first black player."

"What are you talking about? Not all of us are like that. We've had black players before. Besides I'm the captain. What I say goes," Todd said, winking his eye.

Brandon told him he would come to the tryouts. After all anyone who saw him play would be crazy not to have him on their team. He was a six seven post player who averaged sixteen points, ten rebounds and seven assists last year.

Since Janae and Ms. Odell were still out, Brandon made his own dinner then went to bed early.

———————

Six o'clock the next morning, Janae had gotten ready for work while Brandon paced the floor.

"Nervous?" she asked, headed for the door.

"Not really."

She kissed his cheek. "I'm leaving baby. Remember, I'll probably get home late since we have that big meeting, so you go ahead and eat without me. And remember, don't let anyone get to you today. You belong there just as much as they do," she said, giving him another peck on the cheek. She took three steps then came back into Brandon's room. "Oh and remember…"

"Ma. Not another kiss. Will you please go to work? I'll be alright."

Janae laughed. "I was just going to tell you that I left you some money on the kitchen table and Ms. Odell has breakfast ready for you smarty pants."

"Thanks!" Brandon said with a slight smile.

After getting dressed, Brandon ran downstairs to eat. He was in the middle of his second helping of eggs when he heard the door bell ring.

"I'll get it! You finish eating," Ms. Odell sang.

Brandon kept eating. He was almost finished when Todd walked in the kitchen. "Dude, let's go. You don't want to be late on your first day do you?"

"Is the bus here?" Brandon asked.

"The bus is for losers."

"I guess I'm one of those losers cause' I have to catch the bus."

"No you don't," Todd said, throwing a set of keys up in the air. "You're riding with me."

"Cool, let's go."

As Brandon was gathering his belongings, Todd complimented him on his outfit.

"What kind of shirt is that? I've never seen that before," Todd said impressed.

"It's Blac Label."

Todd shook his head with approval and headed to the front door.

Brandon grabbed his back pack and followed Todd to a black BMW that was parked in their driveway.

"Shorty, your moms let you drive her car?"

"Dude, this is my ride."

"What?"

"Yeah, I got it for my sixteenth birthday. It was a gift from my dad. It's kind of a pity gift. He feels like crap for leaving us for this blond, bombshell in his office."

"Whoa. I thought I had problems with my pops," Brandon said feeling sorry for Todd. "Shorty, don't sweat it. My pops left when he found out my moms was pregnant. He'll be back when he see me signing that multi million dollar contract."

"That's the same way I feel. And you know what I'm going to tell him."

"Sorry sucker!"

The two laughed.

Brandon wasn't used to hanging out with any new people. Ever since he was younger, it was always just him, T-Bone, Ray-Ray, and Dashawn when he was alive. That cut down on all the problems. However, there was something about Todd. Even though he had money, he was down to earth. Then there was the race issue that Todd didn't seem to notice. If he did, it didn't bother him that he and Brandon were from two totally different backgrounds.

They drove about two miles before they got to the school's security gate. As they drove past the gate, Brandon was in awe. The school looked more like a resort than a high school. It had a large courtyard with a sitting area lined with shade trees, beautifully landscaped lawns, two baseball fields, a lake, and a college sized football stadium.

The school itself was a huge three story beautiful glass structure that looked foreign to Brandon. Most of the kids were driving luxury cars. The kids who didn't drive were brought to school by a parent who was driving a nice car.

"Shorty, this place is off the hook," Brandon said, looking at the buildings as they passed them.

"It's alright. Wait 'til you see the gym. It has a state

of the art weight room, Jacuzzi tub, and an Olympic size pool."

They pulled up at the main building where most of the classes were held.

"What's your first class?" Todd asked, taking off his seat belt.

"Um…let me see," Brandon said, pulling out his schedule. "It's honors biology."

"I have honors bio too. I have Mrs. Freedomburg."

"So do I," Brandon said excited. "At least I won't be in class with a bunch of strangers."

Brandon and Todd walked into the school's front door. Todd was very popular so he was immediately greeted by everyone. Brandon on the other hand was given strange looks, instead of high-fives. This infuriated Todd.

"Hey, this is my boy, Brandon," he said to a group of his friends. "You mess with him and you'll have to deal with me."

Brandon was surprised. He couldn't believe Todd would go to bat for him like that after only knowing him for two days.

One of Todd's friends came over first to introduce himself to Brandon.

"Hey,what's up dude? I'm Frankie."

"What's up shorty?" Brandon replied.

"Frankie's on the basketball team too," Todd said. "Brandon's gonna try out today."

"Cool beans! We need someone on the inside to stop that kid from Washington High."

"They're our rivals," Todd explained to Brandon. "Hey we better get to class. Mrs. Freedomburg can be a real pain when you're late."

The two boys strolled down the hall to their class. When Brandon had to duck to get into the class, a few kids started laughing. Brandon was used to the stares and giggles, so it didn't bother him. He just walked in and sat down. Mrs. Freedomburg welcomed the kids back from their winter break, and then introduced Brandon to the class before starting her lesson.

The same scenario happened in each of Brandon's classes so he was glad when the last bell rang. When he stepped out of his class, Todd was waiting for him.

"So how was your first day?" Todd asked.

"It went better than I thought. I think after everyone got over the initial shock of having a new black kid in their class it was alright. I did see two other blacks today. My mom told me we make up only three percent of the school's population. "

"Don't worry. They'll warm up to you, especially when they see you on the court. You might even be more popular than I am."

"I doubt that very seriously," Brandon said laughing.

━━━━━━━━━━

Once Brandon and Todd changed their clothes in the locker room they headed out to the court. As soon as the coach laid eyes on Brandon, he knew they had a chance to win the championship. He walked over to Brandon.

"Hi, I'm Coach Matthews. I'm glad to finally meet you," he said, shaking Brandon's hand.

"Excuse me. How do you know me?"

"I've been watching you since you were in middle school. When they told me you were coming to St. Mary's, I thought they were joking. But here you are?"

"Yes, thanks to me," Todd said, putting his arm around the coach. "You can thank me later."

Coach Matthews shook his head. "Oh God, don't tell

me you know this trouble-maker already."

"We're actually neighbors," Brandon replied.

"Well, don't let him get you into any trouble," Coach Matthews said, smiling.

Todd introduced Brandon to a few of the fellows before try outs began. Minutes later, Coach Matthews told the guys to line up.

"Welcome back fellas. I'll be picking players for our J.V. and Varsity squads, so good luck." He clapped his hands together, quickly and loudly. "Let's get this party started!"

Coach Matthews was a very competitive man. For the last three years, his team always made it to the playoffs, but never made it past that. He was determined this year to win the State Championship.

"Okay, guys, let's start off with some warm-ups, then I want you to break off into five teams."

After two hours of working on offensive and defensive drills, Coach Matthews told the guys to line up.

"Thank you all for coming out today. I will have a list posted tomorrow with the names of the players that made the team. If your name is on the list, I expect to see you Friday at three o clock for our first official practice."

The guys went to the locker rooms to change before they headed home. Brandon and Todd stayed behind. Sitting on the bleachers, they got to know each other better.

"So, Todd, what does your moms do for a living?"

"Besides living off my dad, she's a District Manager for a chain of specialty stores. What about your mother?"

"She's the VP for a big Marketing firm in D.C.," Brandon said with pride. "She started in the mailroom and worked her way up."

"That's awesome!"

"It seems you're very popular with the girls at school," Brandon said to Todd.

"I guess."

"What about you?" Todd asked.

Brandon laughed. "I'm gonna tell you something, but if you repeat it I'm gonna kick your butt."

Todd was intrigued. "What?"

"Everyone in my old neighborhood thought I was the man. They have no idea I'm the only virgin left in America."

"Dude…no way!"

"Yeah, see my man got AIDS when he was fifteen, and I definitely don't want to end up like him."

"Wow, that's deep," Todd said, shaking his head.

The two boys talked for over an hour as if they'd known each other for years. Finally they'd talked themselves silly, so they decided to drive home.

When Todd pulled his BMW into the driveway at his house, he asked Brandon, "Hey, you want to go to the mall after school tomorrow?"

"Sure, which mall?"

"Tyson's Corner. They just opened a new section and I want to see what stores they have."

"Sounds good," Brandon said, stepping out of the car.

Todd and Brandon gave each other high five before heading into their homes.

＊＊＊

The next morning when Brandon woke up, he got dressed quickly, ran down for breakfast then met Todd by his car.

"Dude, today is the day. First we're going to find out who's on the team, and then we're going to go to the mall and check out some chicks."

"I can't wait," Brandon said.

As soon as Todd and Brandon got to school, they took

off toward Coach Matthew's office to see who made the team. When they saw their names, they gave each other some dap. Not only had they both made the team, but Todd was named Captain and Brandon was named Co-Captain.

"Shorty, you know me being Co-Captain is going to ruffle some feathers," Brandon said with concern. "I'm the new blood around here."

"Dude, who cares. If they have a problem with it they can always find another team to play for. "Besides, you may be new blood, but you're the best blood."

"I guess." Brandon shrugged his shoulders then threw his backpack on.

Todd and Brandon breezed through their first four classes, then met up for lunch.

"Hey what are you going to eat," Todd said, looking at the menu.

"Umm…I'm not sure."

They finally decided on pizza and fries. After paying for the food, they walked over to the table where the rest of Todd's friends were. As they got closer to the table, Brandon overheard one of the guys complaining.

"He's been here all of what…twenty-four hours and he's already trying to take over our team. Next, we're going to have to go out together for fried chicken and start calling each other "shorty" after the game," the curly head guy said. The small crowd at the table laughed. "Or we're going to have replace Gatorade for Kool-Aid."

Brandon sat his tray down on the table. Pissed, he walked over to the guy and looked down at him. "What you say?" Brandon asked with his face balled up.

The guy stood up. "You heard me."

"Listen shorty, you don't wanna see me," Brandon said, stepping toward him.

"Dude, I'm not scared of you," he said, although he

was visibly shaken, "or all that fancy, slick talk."

"Well you should be," Brandon replied, jumping at him.

The guy was so scared he ducked.

Todd grabbed Brandon around the waist. "Don't do it. He's not worth it!"

The crowd was quiet until Todd started laughing at the guy. "Lunch cost $3.00…the look on your face… priceless," he said, laughing even harder.

Brandon sat down next to Todd and tried to eat his lunch, but he was too upset. He'd lived in D.C. around his own kind his whole life so he never really understood what people meant when they would say racism still existed in America. That was until today. Racism had smacked him dead in the face and he didn't like it.

"Don't let those jerks get to you man," Todd said, trying to comfort Brandon.

"How can I not? I'm not used to people hating on me, because I'm black."

"It's not a black or white thing. He's just mad, because you're the Co-Captain. You got skills, man."

"Where have you been for the last thirty minutes? Did you hear what he said?"

Todd sat in silence for a few minutes before speaking. "Maybe you're right. I just hope you don't think I'm that way, because I hang out with them. I mean seriously…I didn't even know you were black until you told me."

Brandon cracked a smile, but he was still upset about the situation.

After lunch, Brandon and Todd headed to their next class. Brandon tried hard to pay attention to what his teacher was saying, but he couldn't concentrate. *Come on B. This is exactly what they want. Don't let them get to you like this,* he thought to himself. So he put all the nonsense behind him, and focused on his schoolwork.

When the bell rang for dismissal, Brandon strolled to his locker as if no one else existed. He grabbed his coat and waited for Todd outside. As he waited for Todd, he noticed a beautiful mixed girl with curly black hair and Indian features. *I wonder if they bother her,* he thought. *Probably not, she looks more white than black. Nooooooo, I take that back, he thought looking at her again.* He laughed at himself.

"She's hot…huh," Todd said, startling Brandon.

"She's alright."

"Dude, who says that? She's more than alright. She's fine."

Brandon opened the door to the BMW. "Shorty, I got my mind on basketball and my money. Chicks can wait!"

"So what? You don't plan on dating anyone?"

"I didn't say that." Brandon fastened his seatbelt. "Todd, being in a relationship is hard. I mean, what's the one thing girls yell about us not doing?"

Todd scratched his head. "I don't know…remembering their birthday?"

"Man, come on! You know the answer…We don't spend time with them."

Todd laughed. "I knew that," he said, turning on the ramp to Highway 395.

"Well, when you have practice four days a week, games on Friday nights, and Saturday morning team meetings, you don't have a lot of time to spend with a girlfriend."

"Trust me. I would make time for one!" Todd said laughing.

═══════════════

Finding a parking spot was almost impossible. After circling the mall a few times, Todd got lucky and found a spot not far from one of the main doors. They got out and walked through the mall's North entrance.

"So what are you getting?" Todd asked Brandon.

"Joe, these designers don't make clothes to fit me."

"Who's Joe?"

Brandon snickered. "Joe is another word for Dude."

"Oh…okay Joe," Todd said, trying to sound hip. "I'm quite sure there's something in here you can wear."

"I doubt it. Besides I only wear clothes by All Daz, Shooters, and Visionz." Brandon could tell Todd was lost so he explained to him that they were urban labels designed by D.C. based designers. "I like shorts that stop just above my knees, not cradle up my butt cheeks."

"It's cool. We all have our differences. I like my hair spiked with extra spritz, while you wear braids. You wear long shorts. I like Bermuda's." He laughed. "But we both can play some hoops."

Todd stopped to make a fake dunk with an imaginary ball.

"C'mon dude. Let's go look at some stores in the new section of the mall. Maybe you'll find those shorts you're looking for."

Brandon shook his head. "If you say so."

"Okay…well I'm going into Neiman's. I want to see if they have any new Ed Hardy shirts."

Todd was the first through the door at Neiman's. As soon as he entered the men's department a saleswoman greeted him. Brandon, who walked in right behind him, received nothing. Not a hello, not a wave, nothing…just a snobbish stare at his braids. Brandon brushed it off at first. *Maybe she didn't see me. What the heck am I saying? How could she not see me, I'm six foot seven.*

"This shirt is hot," Todd said with excitement. "I'm going to go try it on."

"Knock yourself out. I'll go look around until you come out."

"Cool beans dude," Todd said, walking to the dressing rooms.

While Todd tried on his shirt, Brandon looked around. As he walked around, he noticed a security officer following him. To see if he was right, he played a little game of cat and mouse with the officer. He walked up one side of the store, cut through, then walked to the other side. The officer was still watching him. *Let me test this guy,* he thought. He quickly grabbed a couple of shirts off the table and walked to the dressing room. Just as he was about to walk into the dressing room, the saleswoman immediately asked if he needed any help. *Oh, now you want to speak to me.* She looked inside one of the rooms to make sure it was clear. Then she tried to take the shirts from Brandon.

"Let me put those in there for you."

"I got it," he said, holding the shirts tightly.

Todd heard Brandon's voice and called out to him.

"Did you find something?"

Brandon smiled at the clerk. "I sure did," he said, going into the fitting room.

Todd emerged from the dressing room first. "I'll take this," he told the clerk.

"Okay sir, I'll be right with you. I just have to wait for another customer to come out," she said, trying to look under the door of Brandon's dressing room.

Todd waited. As he was waiting, he noticed the clerk and the security officer whispering and pointing at Brandon's dressing room.

"Hey, what's going on?"

The clerk turned to him. "Nothing, I'll be right with you," she said, standing guard at the dressing room door.

Just then Brandon walked out.

"I ain't no thief. As a matter of fact, if I wanted to, I could buy those shirts and anything else I wanted in this store." After telling them both off, he threw the shirts at them and stormed off. Todd did the same.

"Dude, can you believe that?"

"What are you talkin' bout? Yeah, I can believe it. It seems to be the norm around this camp; seems like the rich Virginia folks have this mentality that black people steal. It never crosses their mind that we can actually afford nice clothes. And most of us are hard working people."

"Oh God…hear we go again. Brandon, did it occur to you that maybe it was, because we are dressed like bums in these sweats and dirty t-shirts… and not because you're black?"

"If that's the case, then why did she speak to you and not me? Why didn't the security officer follow you around? Why didn't she stand guard outside your door? I don't care how we looked, we have the right to shop in here and not be harassed just like anybody else. You need to get your head out of the sand man."

"You know what…you're right… screw this place man. You're my friend and nobody's going to treat you badly while I'm around."

Brandon had made a valid point. So, they both left the mall without buying anything.

Three weeks later, on a Friday night, the gym was packed. It was the team's first game, and to top it off, it was against their rival, Martinsville High, who they could never seem to beat. The guys were hyped. It was Brandon's debut, and he was nervous. There was so much talk about how well he could play, so he felt like he had to live up to everyone's expectations of him. He was going to need all the support he could get so he invited his boys T-Bone and Ray-Ray to the game. He'd already asked his mother if they could ride to the game with her, and spend the night afterwards.

The band started playing and one by one the players ran out on the court. In the middle of the court, they huddled up and chanted. "Bulldogs...Bulldogs...Bulldogs," they yelled, swaying from side to side.

The emcee began announcing the starters as the crowd cheered loudly. When they announced Brandon's name, his mother, T-Bone, and Ray-Ray jumped to their feet screaming at the top of their lungs, "Yeeeeaaaaa...go Brandon."

Brandon instantly became nervous, wondering how his school-mates would react to Ray-Ray with his 70's bush, and the huge pick stuck in his hair. Not to mention the numerous chains T-Bone wore, drooped outside his sweater.

To Brandon's surprised the crowd roared too and chanted along with Ray-Ray. *Now I really got to bring my A game, he thought.* As he and Todd stood in the middle of floor greeting the referees and the Captain and Co-Captain from Martinsville, they could hear the crowd yelling their names. Brandon was finally starting to feel like he belonged at St. Mary's.

The buzzer sounded warning the teams that it was game time. Brandon took center stage against the post player from Martinsville. With a four inch height advantage over him, he jumped and smacked the ball to their end of the court. Todd took it in for a lay up. The gym rocked as the spectators went wild.

In the last quarter of the game, St. Mary's had a three point lead over Martinsville, but after their star player shot a three pointer the game was tied.

The crowd started yelling, "Defense...Defense...Defense."

The coach called his last time out with 10 seconds left in the game.

"Guys, I want you to stack up. Frankie, I need you to throw the ball to either Todd or Brandon, who will break away to mid court. Guys, I need you to score, or draw a foul. Okay! Hands in. One…two…three…"

"Teamwork," the players yelled.

Frankie did just as the coach asked. He threw the ball to Brandon who was mid court. When Brandon turned around, he had a Martinsville player right up on him. *This fool must don't know who I am,* he thought as he gave him his famous crossover pump fake move. Once the player was shaken, Brandon dunked the ball with both hands right at the buzzer. The crowd went wild. It was over. St. Mary's had beaten Martinsville for the first time in ten years. With a score of 87-85, the crowd began a chant that sounded sweet to Brandon's heart.

"Brandon, Brandon, Brandon," they cheered in unison.

═══════════════

The team was on cloud nine when they entered the locker room. Frankie approached Brandon, and immediately reached out for a hand shake.

Hey dude, we're going to Sparky's to celebrate. You and your boys wanna come? They look pretty cool."

Brandon wanted to spend some time with his boys, so he didn't go with the rest of the team. He and Todd decided to go to Brandon's house to hang out with T-Bone and Ray-Ray.

Sitting in Brandon's family room, the boys got caught up on all the Norteast D.C. gossip.

"Shorty, did you know Jo-Jo was dating Dawn?" T-Bone asked.

"That roller," Brandon replied.

He looked at Todd, because he knew he didn't understand what they were talking about. "A roller is a girl who sleeps around with a lot of guys," he said schooling Todd.

"Ooohhh...then why is he dating her?"

Ray-Ray and T-Bone simply laughed.

The guys were getting hungry, so Brandon asked Ms. Odell if she would make them something to eat. A half an hour later, Ms. Odell returned to the family room with sandwiches and drinks for everyone.

"Would you like anything else Brandon?" Ms. Odell asked.

"No Ma'am. Thank you," he said smiling.

T-Bone and Ray-Ray were in awe.

"Dang nigga. It must be nice to have someone waitin' on you hand and foot," T-Bone said, slapping Brandon on the head. "Will there be anything else Master Brandon?" he asked, mocking Ms. Odell.

"Y'all niggas crazy. It ain't even like that. Ms. Odell's like family."

Every time Todd heard one of the guys use the word nigga, his face would become flush. He was expecting someone to start fighting. He had always been taught that the word was offensive and used to degrade African Americans, but Brandon and his friends were saying it, and it didn't seem to bother them.

Soon, the boys finished their sandwiches. "What ya'll wanna do now?" Brandon asked, after taking his last sip of tea.

"Throw in that Martin Lawrence joint," T-Bone demanded, taking off his sneakers to get comfortable.

"A'ight," Brandon said, standing up and walking over to his massive collection of DVD movies. "Let me see if I can find it."

As Brandon looked for the DVD, Todd, Ray-Ray, and

T-Bone got better acquainted. Ray-Ray stood up and walked over to Brandon.

"Hey…B…yo boy Todd's kinda cool for a white boy."

"No doubt, he's been helping me out a lot. You know, helping at school and introducing me to people. He even stood up for me when we went shopping and this butt hole security officer was following me around like I was trying to steal or something."

"That's love man!"

Brandon waved the DVD in his hand. "I found it!"

He popped the DVD in and took a seat on the couch next to his friends.

Laughing so hard, they were almost choking. The boys fell over one another as Martin Lawrence told his famous Ham and Cheese joke.

"That nigga crazy! I'm telling you, can't nobody mess with him man. He got the comedy thing on lock," Ray-Ray said, laughing hysterically.

"Shorty, you ain't never lied," T-Bone replied.

As the credits rolled, Brandon cleaned up their mess, then broke the bad news to his friends that he was tired and wanted to go to bed.

"Nigga, stop acting like an old man," Ray-Ray said laughing.

"Ain't nobody acting like an old man. Did you forget I had a game tonight?"

"You right…my bad shorty."

Todd got up. "Well, I'm headed home. I'm a little tired myself."

"A'ight shorty. It was nice to meet you and thanks for having my nigga's back," T-Bone said, giving Todd some dap.

"Yeah…good looking out," Ray-Ray said.

"No problem," Todd said, walking out the room. "I'll check you nigga's later."

The room fell silent. It was like Todd had sucked the air out of it.

"What did you say?" Brandon asked, swelling up.

Todd was baffled. "I said I'll see you nigga's la…"

Brandon's fist immediately connected to Todd's right cheek. Todd fell to the ground taking Janae's bookcase with him. The commotion caused Ms. Odell to awaken from her sleep and run down the hallway to the family room.

"Brandon…what's going on?" Ms. Odell yelled, pushing him back.

"He just called us niggas," Brandon said, trying to get to Todd.

"Cut it out! You get back." She went over and examined Todd's bleeding mouth. "All of you sit down," she yelled, as she got a napkin for Todd's mouth.

The boys sat down one by one. Brandon, T-Bone, and Ray-Ray stared at Todd.

"I should break you up! How are you gonna come up in my crib and call me a nigga?" Brandon asked while fuming. He wanted to hit Todd again.

Ms. Odell turned to Todd. "Is that true young man?"

"Yes, Ma'am, but I…"

"But nothing punk. I ain't no nigga!" Brandon yelled, lashing out at Todd.

"Brandon, I'll handle this," Ms. Odell said. She sat down next to Todd. "Why would you call someone who you consider a friend something so ugly?"

With his eyes blood shot red, and one side of his face blackish-blue, Todd looked over at Brandon. "I didn't mean it that way. I heard you, T-Bone, and Ray-Ray saying it so I thought it was okay. I even heard you saying it a few times when it was just the two of us," he added. "You say the word so casually, I thought it was okay!"

"It's okay for us to say it, but it ain't okay for you to

say it," Brandon yelled.

Ms. Odell sat back on the couch. "Umm…now I see what the problem is." She told the boys to listen to her. "Brandon why is it acceptable for you and your friends to use the N-word, but it's not okay for Todd to use it."

Brandon sighed deeply before answering. "Because when we say it, we're saying it in a friendly way."

Ms. Odell was disgusted. "Sweetie, that word is a hideous racial slur created to degrade Black people. There's no place for it in our culture and I don't care how it's used, it's still a negative and cruel word. You young fellows sit around using the word as a term of endearment, but when Todd used the word you saw it as a form of disrespect. If you don't want him to disrespect you, why don't you set an example and not use it yourselves? There are plenty of other choices of words you can use to let someone know they're your boy. Try deleting the word from your vocabulary."

The boys sat for a few more minutes and listened to Ms. Odell school them.

"Brandon you're my friend. I swear I didn't mean to hurt you. I just wanted to fit in with you guys. So, when I heard you guys saying it, without killing each other, I thought it was okay," Todd admitted.

Brandon sat and thought about what Ms. Odell said, and agreed with her. He couldn't fault Todd for using the word when he himself had used the word many times. So, he apologized to Todd. He then vowed to never use the word again. T-Bone made the same promise, but Ray-Ray said he wasn't so sure he could kick the habit.

"I'll try," he muttered.

For years, people like Martin Luther King, Thurgood Marshall, Rosa Parks, and Medger Evers were subjected to being beaten and jailed, so African-Americans could have the right to vote and be treated equally. They've endured being called a "nigger" in a way that is undignified and here we are today using the word carelessly. I often wonder what they would think about our young black men calling each other, "NIGGA."

Teenage Bluez

TRUTH BEHIND LIES

by Lakeyshia Dorsey

"What do you want?" Ericka asked with attitude, as she stood inside her doorway.

The two-story house sat on the corner of Mosher and Bent, which proved to be an open target for nosy neighbors.

"Ericka, you didn't even tell me what happ…"

Ericka stepped onto the front porch and allowed the screen door to shut slowly behind her. She prayed her mother wouldn't hear her and come fussing about her talking to Derrick.

"A few Baltimore police cops informed me up about you, Derrick. They said that they saw me handle some of your 'equipment' or something like that. They had me in that station for hours!" She crossed her arms with even more sass than before. "This is my senior year, Derrick. I can't miss time from school like that," she said cutting him off.

Derrick had been her boyfriend for a little over a year, and still hadn't gotten rid of his thug boy lifestyle. The relationship had been rocky, yet Ericka continued to give their dating a shot.

"I know, but listen…I'm going to call Boss about those cops. He knows all of them….so he'll take care of that, seriously."

"Ummm…huh. I bet."

Derrick continued… "But even still they had to be bluffing you out. I mean you didn't do anything so just chill."

"Whatever Derrick. Everybody is always telling me how much trouble you are, but do I listen? No! Sometimes I wonder why I even bother with you." she said, out of anger.

Derrick stood on the porch towering over Ericka's unique frame. At 5'5 most would've coined her as petite, however, Ericka was thick to be seventeen, and possessed the muscles of someone who worked out daily. She wasn't as curvaceous as the other girls she hung out with, but her silky hair and, perfectly tanned complexion made up for any disinterest one would have from the physical looks of her body.

"You love me don't you?" he asked.

"I hate when you ask me that question."

"Ericka, I have to do what I have to do. I can't help it."

"I know, I know it's in your blood right?" Ericka replied. "Well, being drug free is in mine!"

"I don't do drugs either!" Derrick shouted.

"Yeah…but you sell them. Don't lie. I know you do," she ended with a frown on her face. "When are you going to stop selling drugs, Derrick?"

Derrick just stared at her, as she rolled her honey brown eyes. No matter what, her face always seemed to make him smile. Maybe it was her dimples, or maybe the way she let her long ponytail swing to the side of her head like an innocent little girl.

"Why do you always get so mad with me?" he asked.

"Derrick…I'm not mad with you. I'm just frustrated."

"Why?"

"You always expect people to understand why you do things that you know are wrong. But when the time comes for somebody to tell you anything, you just blow them off."

"Baby, you're just overprotective of me."

"It's more than that. I'm tired of the excuse that's it's in your blood. Your father sold drugs and now he has life in prison. Is that what you want for yourself?"

"C'mon Ericka," Derrick whined while shaking his head.

"It's not that deep in your blood if Darius not doing it," she added.

Darius was Derrick's identical twin brother. The only difference in their looks was that Derrick had a scar under his left eye that he received in a gang fight. They were both on the high end of the light-skinned brotha club.

"Oh, Boy. Here we go with this again. Why do you always have to go there? He's him and I'm me."

"I know that, but you're smart, Derrick, very smart, and you're just throwing it all away. Darius has a good job, he's starting college in the fall, and he's got his own place. Now remember, he's nineteen just like you, so if he can break the family curse, you can too."

"Why do you always have to do this?" Derrick ranted. "You always putting all this pressure and stress on me!"

"You don't think you stress me out too? You're always fighting, gone half the night, and I never know where you are or what you're doing. I'm only seventeen years old, and too young to be stressed out. You wouldn't have to worry about me fussing if you stop what you are doing and get yourself together."

"Whatever," he said.

"And now you're blowing me off. Why can't you just listen to what I say!" Ericka screamed.

She was so frustrated with Derrick, but she also had so much love for him as well. Ericka started to walk away from him but Derrick grabbed her by the arm.

"Get off me," she said snatching away from him.

"No, come here." He pulled her 120 lb frame easily back toward him, he then placed a kiss on her lips. Their arguments always ended this way. Ericka could never resist his pretty boy looks, with his lightly freckled skin and wavy hair. But his thuggish ways would have to stop.

"Whatever," she said as she pushed him off the step

and rushed to re-open her front door. "I gotta go."

"Ericka!" Derrick called out to her.

"What?"

"Do you still love me?" He smiled widely.

"Yes, I love you," she said. *And it kills me every day,* she thought as she shut the door behind her.

Ericka was a senior who'd been making straight A's for years. In addition to that she was envied by most girls, because of her beauty and her confidence. Although Ericka had an athletic body, she was still a girlie girl, loving her entourage of colorful lip glosses.

Overall, she truly cared about people's feelings, yet she always spoke what was on her mind. She was a tough girl when she needed to be, especially when hanging with her crew. Whenever you saw Ericka at school you were sure to see her home girl Tina, and possibly her other two hanging buddies. Although they primarily hung out on the weekends, they were also a close knit dance group.

Without a doubt, they were one of the best B-more had to offer. Competition after competition, they'd enter and win, and battled any dance group that came their way. Ironically, Ericka met Derrick two years ago at club Paradox at one of those competitions. Immediately after she and her friends tore up the dance floor against a group of girls from Prince Georges County, she noticed Derrick staring at her.

Ericka being the ring leader of her friends and Derrick being the ring leader of his click, they quickly clicked together at first sight. Soon after they started talking, Ericka quickly learned how much of a bad boy that Derrick really was. She learned things about him that she didn't like. He was a gang banger and was hanging out with a rough group of boys. She was so confident that she could change him, she proceeded with the relationship. Over time, he slowed down a bit, but never stopped. And Ericka found herself wrapped around his finger.

"Girl, who was you out there talking to?" her mother asked as she entered the living room.

"Ahh….Ahh…"

"Aahhh…nothing," she responded sarcastically. "And why you got tears in your eyes? I know you not crying over some lil' pea head boy."

"I don't understand it either Ma. I know I shouldn't," she admitted.

"Is it Derrick?"

Ericka just shook her head.

"I told you countless times to leave him alone, Ericka. He's not worth it."

"I know Ma, but it's not that easy," she sniffled.

"You gonna learn the hard way….just watch," she ended.

Even though Ericka never really got along with her alcoholic mother after her father left them, she still didn't like to argue with her. She knew that a life with Derrick was not good for her, but she needed to end the conversation with her mother. She'd been drinking again and would reveal many more horrible stories to Ericka about her father half the night if she didn't let it go.

"I understand Ma," she finally said, making her way toward the steps leading to her room.

"Remember, that boy almost got you beat up once before, and you still following him around like a lost puppy."

"I gotta study!" she yelled from the top of the stairs.

Ericka closed her ears, because she didn't want to hear anymore derogatory remarks about Derrick. She closed her door, and pressed her face into her pillow.

The next day at school, Ericka rushed to the cafeteria to meet Tina. Tina was the tallest of the crew, and definitely possessed the loudest mouth. Ericka could see her making her way over to her.

"Hey girl," Tina said loudly as she walked up to Ericka popping gum. You didn't have to watch them long to know they were best friends. They'd known each other the longest of all the four girls in the dance group, and had the most in common.

"What's up?" Ericka replied.

"Nothin' much. What happened to you on yesterday, you didn't even come to school?"

"Oh, I came but Derrick had me caught up with some mess. The police came to school during first period to talk to me."

"Oh my God! Not again." She rolled her eyes in frustration, and made a loud popping sound with her gum.

"Girl, I don't even want to talk about it."

"I feel you," Tina said pulling out a file to file her nail. "Hey, Ericka, do you know him?" She pointed with her chipped nail.

"Who?"

"That boy at that table over there." She kept pointing.

When Ericka finally turned to see who Tina was talking about, she noticed a light-skinned boy staring at her from across the room.

"No, I've never seen him before," Ericka replied. "But he's light, just like I like'em." She laughed.

"Well, he sure does know you," Tina said in a not so funny tone.

Ericka looked over at him again. She could see that he was talking to a boy next to him and pointing her way. She didn't know who he was, but it looked pretty suspicious to her.

"Come on, I'm ready to go," Ericka said.

"If you say so," Tina uttered. "Just think, he's sitting near the only doors we can go out of. But, let's go." She took a deep breath. "Oh, what about Michelle, and Stacy?"

"Who cares," Ericka responded almost in a daze.

"Alright, I'll just call them on the cell, and tell'em to meet us at your locker."

"Please do, 'cause I don't like this guy staring at me."

"Look at you, he got you all paranoid. It's that dog'on Derrick. He's into so much bad stuff, now he's got you looking out to make sure that nobody's going to bank you, or shoot you."

Tina chuckled, then allowed her finger nail file to go to work once again. They both started walking in the direction of the exit doors of the cafeteria.

"Well, I got you so I don't have to worry about getting banked," Ericka joked, while keeping one eye on her stalker.

Tina laughed at her just as they started to walk out the huge double doors. Before they could get ten feet away, someone called Ericka by her name. She stopped in her tracks, then turned completely around.

"Ericka, isn't that your name?" the voice said.

Ericka and Tina looked at one another, then back at the light-skinned boy who was now close enough for them to sneak a detailed view. He sat on the edge of a chair, backwards, as if he had no home training at all.

"Why do you want to know my name?" Ericka questioned.

"Cause I want to know," the boy stated.

"Well, who are you?" she asked.

"I'm a friend of your boyfriend," he said standing and moving closer to her.

Ericka appeared to be shook for a moment. There was

something about his eyes that held her hostage. They were green, money green, sorta hypnotizing. "Well, you must be mistaken, because I don't have a boyfriend," she said backing away.

"Wait a minute. So you're telling me-you don't go with Derrick?" he questioned.

"No, I don't," she said quickly, then walked away with Tina hot on her heels. She knew it had something to do with Derrick, and couldn't wait to drill him.

As soon as Ericka stuck her key in her front door, she rushed over to the cordless phone, dialed Derrick's number, and started shouting into the phone.

"Wait…slow down…what happened?" Derrick asked.

" I saidddddddddddd! A boy came up to me in school, he knew my name, and he knew I knew you. He didn't even go to my school!" Ericka shouted.

"How do you know that?" Derrick asked calmly.

"Trust me, Tina didn't know him, and Tina knows everybody."

Ericka paced the floors with nervousness.

"What did he say to you babe?"

"Well, at first he didn't say anything. He was just eye-balling me. Then he called my name on the way out the door. When I asked him who he was, he said he was a friend of my boyfriend. When I said I didn't have a boyfriend, he asked me did I go with you."

Derrick remained quiet for a minute. Ericka didn't know if he was thinking or asleep. As usual, he'd probably stayed up half the night, and wasn't rested up yet.

"What did he look like?" Derrick asked after a few

seconds of silence. "Umm…he was light-skinned, kind of tall, slim, long braids… and I could never forget those green eyes," she said slowly.

"Did you say green eyes?" Derrick asked in shock.

"Yeah, I could never forget."

"I'll call you right back, I'm going to check out something," Derrick told her in a weird voice.

Ericka waited all night for her return phone call, but as usual Derrick's priority was running the streets. The next morning she woke up feeling uneasy. Derrick hadn't followed through with the green eye search, which made her wish she could've stayed home.

By the time she made it to school, she seemed to be in a daze. Throughout the day nothing changed, but the three quizzes she took kept her mind focused for a while. Knowing that she had dance practice after school, she tried to regain her confident composure near the end of the day. As soon as Tina walked up to her in the locker room, she bombarded her with questions, "Did you ask him? What did he say? Did he know the guy? "

"Well…hi to you too, Tina. I'm fine, and you."

They both laughed, including Michelle and Stacy.

"I'm sorry but I want to know," Tina asked again without shame.

"And so do the rest of us," Michelle said, as she popped her bubblegum. Michelle was the shortest out of the bunch standing at 5'0. She was also the quiet one of the bunch who preferred to dance instead of talk. The girls needed to meet badly so they could practice some new dance moves. The school was having a pep rally, just two days away, and they were performing in it along with a couple other dance groups. They had to be ready so they could be the best.

"Well, my little nosy friends, yes I did ask Derrick if

he knew anything about my fine stalker. He didn't say whether or not he knew the boy," Ericka stated. "He said he would call me back."

"What do you mean?" Stacy asked, as she started stretching. Stacy always led the stretches. It was a habit, plus she wanted the girls to maintain their athletic bodies.

Ericka got down on the floor and spread her legs widely. As she stretched, she made excuses for Derrick. "It's cool…I mean that he just said that he was going to check something out. That's it. I mean he did get kind of uneasy when I said the guy had these striking green eyes," Ericka explained.

"Sounds shady to me," Tina interjected.

"I don't know." Ericka hunched her shoulders. "Well, he'll call me. If he doesn't, then I'll call his brother, Darius."

"I hear he is fineeeeeeee," Michelle sang.

"Not as cute as my man," Ericka shot back. "Anyway, lets let's start practicing cause we only got two days," she added, while switching the subject.

"Girl, please. Don't worry," Tina laughed. "We're top dog around here."

———————

Two days passed and Ericka still hadn't heard from Derrick. She'd been so wrapped up in the pep rally preparations that she really hadn't worried about him at all.

It was the day of the pep rally and it was the group's turn to dance. They really weren't talking to each other much. They seemed to be getting mentally prepared to do their thing.

Ericka looked into the stands with a great feeling inside. Everyone was cheering for them. It made her smile to see football players, cheerleaders, popular girls, unpopular ones too, and even teachers clapping for the team. All of a sudden, a frown appeared on her face. Ericka spotted the same boy from the other day. He was in the front row staring straight at her.

Immediately, Ericka became freaked. *"Okay, what's this about?* she wondered.

As the music started, she vowed to put his presence out of her mind. Ericka wasn't going to let him mess up her well known performance. She did look at him though, and sometimes their eyes met and never left each other. At the end of their performance, Ericka took off in his direction. She'd decided to approach him, hoping to get to the bottom of it all, but the stranger was nowhere to be found. Ericka once again put it out of her mind for several minutes.

The group ended up winning the award for Best Dance Squad, like they had done every year for the last four years. The other girls were mad, but hated from the sidelines. Suddenly, Ericka's cell phone rang. She didn't recognize the number. Everything seemed strange. Her heart raced at the thought of the stranger. *Could it have been him? Did he have her phone number?* She hesitated before answering. "Hello."

"Who is it?" Tina asked.

Ericka just hunched her shoulders and repeated herself. "Hello?"

"Baby," the voice said.

"Who is this?" Ericka asked.

"Oh, so you don't know my voice now? It's only been a week," the voice responded.

"Derrick?"

"There we go. How was the pep rally?"

"Is it Derrick?" Tina asked.

Ericka just nodded her head.

"It was good," she replied.

"Did y'all win?"

125

"What do you think?" she asked nonchalantly.

"Oh, yeah ya'll the champs. I forgot for a minute," he said playfully.

"Whose phone are you calling from?" Ericka asked.

"Darius', and don't be calling him either."

"Boy please, don't nobody want your brother."

"Yeah whatever," Derrick said, in a matter of fact tone.

"You need to be more confident. What, did he take one of you girlfriends from you before?"

Ericka finally found some humor in the conversation. Tina laughed with her.

"Who is that laughing at me?" Derrick asked.

Ericka could tell he was mad. That must've meant that the statement about Darius was true. "My right hand girl," she replied. "You know how Tina is. Don't take it personal." Ericka laughed.

"Oh, little miss nosy. I'm telling you… that girl is into everything," Derrick said laughing too.

"Whatever. Did you find out if you knew the guy who was at my school?" she asked.

"Oh…umm…ye-yeah, I did. Look I wanted to take you out tonight."

"That didn't sound too convincing Derrick. I thought I could get a straight answer. Anyway…what did you have in mind?" she asked.

Ericka knew that something was strange about what he had said but she couldn't figure out what it was.

"The movies. That movie that I told you about last week came out two days ago. I want to go see it," Derrick said.

"Okay, I'll go. I don't have no money though."

"Baby, don't even play with me like that. You know that I got you."

"Mmmhmmm…"

"I'll see you around 7:00."

"Okay." she said as they hung up.

"Well, what did he say?" Tina asked.

"He said that you were nosy," Ericka said as she laughed hysterically.

"I know that, but what did he say about knowing the guy? For real Ericka what did he say?"

"He said that he took care of it, but I don't know, I feel kind of funny about it. He said he was going to take me out tonight."

"Are you going?"

"Yeah. Why not?" Ericka replied.

"You are dumber than dumb," Tina ended, and rolled her eyes.

Ericka was a little nervous when Derrick pulled up in his mother's car. Although she had her license, she knew that his had been suspended.

"Derrick, I'm not playing with you, do not speed in this car," she said as she hopped inside.

"Baby relax, its fine. The police can't catch me in this thing anyway," he bragged.

"Should I get out of this car now?"

"Only if I can get a good look at that cute lil' min-skirt you got on," he joked.

"Whatever Derrick." She smiled.

Ericka did make sure that she looked her best before leaving the house. She wore a cute Baby Phat baby doll shirt, and her new Apple Bottom jean mini that Derrick had bought for her weeks ago. She'd won that dance contest hands down and wanted to celebrate with her man. Derrick drove her to the movies safely, and to her surprise she had a great time.

But even still she had this gut feeling that something wasn't right. Derrick seemed to behave strangely most of the night; checking over his shoulder, making secret calls on his cell, and walking speedily to and from the car.

When Derrick stopped at the gas station to get some gas, he mentioned to Ericka that they needed to talk.

"I'll be right back baby," he said quickly, before exiting the car.

"Okay," Ericka replied with frustration.

She watched Derrick go to the gas teller, and then over to the gas pump. When he was done, Derrick was about to get into the car but somebody called out to him.

"Derrick," Ericka called out to him. Quickly she got out the car too, trying to see who had called him. It was dark, and seemed kind of odd that he'd know someone at the gas station. She gave Derrick the eye as he walked toward the voice.

"I'll be right back, baby," he said, as he continued to walk.

Ericka saw a boy in the shadows but couldn't see his face. Something told her it wasn't a good sign. She didn't move away from the car, but continued to watch Derrick's every move. She could see Derrick shake the boy's hand just before he started to talk to him. Soon, Derrick's body language became tense and he started to walk away from the boy. The boy followed, calling him back.

"Get back in the car!" Derricked shouted Ericka's way. She didn't. She couldn't.

Once the boy stepped from the shadows of the huge trash can, Ericka could see his face clearly. It was the boy from school with the scary green eyes.

Oh my God! Please Derrick, just keep walking!"

But Derrick didn't. He stopped walking, and abruptly turned to his associate. The boy had a smug look firmly planted upon his face. He lifted his right hand and shot Derrick one time in the chest.

"DERRICK!" Ericka screamed. She ran over to him in a hurry. It never dawned on her that maybe he'd shoot her too. Immediately, she started screaming, "help....help....please help!"

When she approached Derrick there was blood everywhere. Quickly, she turned to her right to someone running to assist. She turned to her left and the noticed the shooter was gone.

"Oh, God noooooooooooo!" she shouted as she took off her jacket to apply pressure to his gunshot wound.

"SOMEBODY CALL 911! Hold on baby… just hold on. Please God!"

―――――――――――

Thirty minutes later, Ericka's hands shook as she dialed the number. "Hello?"

"Yeah."

"Darius…" Ericka asked.

"Yeah…who is this?"

"It's Ericka."

"Oh…what's up…what's wrong?" he said."You sound sad. Derrick do something to you?"

"It's Derrick…" Her voice was shaky, and he could tell that she had been crying.

"What happened?"

"He…they…I tried to…"

"Come on. Just tell me."

"They shot him. I didn't know what to do." Ericka started to sob uncontrollably.

"Where are you!" he shouted.

"A-a-a-t the hospital."

"What hospital?"

Darius tried not to panic.

"Mercy," Ericka sobbed.

"I'm on my way."

Click.

━━━━━━━━━━━━━━

While Ericka waited for Darius outside the hospital doors, she made the dreadful call to her mother.

"Where are you!" she shouted. "I know you said Derrick was taking you out, but that movie shoulda been over."

"I'm at the hospital with Derrick," she replied.

"What happened?" Her mother almost sounded concerned.

"He was shot."

"It figures. You do wrong, wrong gets done back to you. You don't need to be hanging with that good for nothing boy anyway."

"Ma, all that isn't necessary."

"Don't tell me what's necessary!"

Ericka's head was now pounding. She didn't think she could take it anymore. Meanwhile, Darius had pulled up out front while she was on the phone.

"Ma, I really don't feel like arguing with you right now. I just called, so you wouldn't worry. I guess I'll see you when I get home," she ended.

"No, you won't. I think I need another drink," she blurted out. "I'm going out so I won't be here. But you get your butt in this house within the next twenty minutes."

Ericka tried to respond, but the only thing she heard was click.

Derrick walked up to see tears streaming from Ericka's eyes. "It's gonna be okay," he said in a comforting tone.

"I know….I have so much on my mind right now." She folded her arms and looked downward not wanting Derrick to see the pain in her eyes. "I hope you didn't mind me calling you. I just couldn't get in touch with your mother," she said to Darius as they walked upstairs to the nurse's station on the second floor.

"It's okay. I'm glad you called, 'cause you look terrible….pretty shook up huh?" Ericka followed Darius' eyes. He was referring to her wrinkled shirt covered in blood, and her messy hair that made it look like she'd been in a gang fight.

"How can I help you?" the nurse asked.

"I'm here to see Derrick Wilson," Darius spoke loudly.

"Are you family?" the nurse asked.

"Yeah, I'm his brother. And she's our cousin." Ericka was too wrapped up in her thoughts to realize that he'd lied.

"Here are your visitor's passes. He's in room 232." The nurse stopped to look at her co-worker, then turned back toward Ericka and Derrick. "He's not in good shape so allow him to rest," she said giving them both the evil eye.

━━━━━━━━━━━━━━━

Ericka and Darius walked down the hall looking into every room until they reached 223. Stepping inside, they watched Derrick sleep. He was so heavily sedated that they had him on a respirator to help him breath. He was almost unrecognizable with all the tubes connected to different parts of his body. Ericka had never seen him sleep. He looked so sweet and innocent. His hands lay still by his side and the sheet was pulled just enough to cover his upper torso.

"Ericka what happened?" Darius asked in a soft tone.

"I don't know... it just happened so fast."

Just thinking about what happened brought her to tears. For a second he contemplated reaching out to comfort her. Then he realized he needed to know what happened. Before Darius could ask her again there was a knock at the door.

"Hello, I'm Dr. Brillo," the doctor said, as he walked in briskly. He was an older man with his grays just sprouting from his chin and throughout his head.

"Hello, I'm Darius. I'm Derrick's brother." He extended his hand toward the doctor.

"Okay. And I recognize you. Aren't you the young lady who came in with Derrick?" he said to Ericka.

"Yes," she replied softly.

"Well, just know that if it wasn't for you, he might have died. Derrick was shot in the upper chest region. It missed his lung by two centimeters, which caused a lot of bleeding. If you hadn't put pressure on it like you did, he would have bled to death," Dr. Brillo explained as he showed them both the x-rays. "Has his mother or father been notified yet?"

"Yes sir, my mother is on the way. I called her."

"Great. Tell her this young lady here saved his life."

Ericka smiled to herself at the thought of saving Derrick Now he just needed to save himself once he was back on the streets.

"Is he going to be okay?" Ericka asked.

"Well, he's lost a lot of blood. He needs a blood transfusion," the doctor explained.

"I can give him some blood," Darius interjected, taking off his jacket.

"Well, we need to test you first," the doctor stated.

"Look at me doctor. We're twins, testing is a waste of time," Darius ranted impatiently.

"Sounds good. But it's hospital policy. Follow me," the

doctor said after snapping from a deep thought.

"Ericka just sit here, I'll take you home when I'm finished. Here call my mother." See where she is," Darius said,
handing Ericka his phone.

"Alright." she replied, taking the phone from Darius,
and placing it to her rear.

Two hours later Darius came back to find his mother
and step-father standing over Derrick's bed, watching him
sleep. His mother had obviously been crying from the stained
tears embedded into her face. Ericka was still wide-eyed and
sitting in the chair like a zombie next to his bed.

"Hey Ma," Darius said as he kissed his mother on the
cheek. "Can you believe this?"

"I just thank God he's alive. And I'm thankful for Ericka."

"Me too," Darius added.

"Yeah, she's a good girl. Why is she with my bad
son?" His mother laughed lightly as she tenderly rubbed the
side of Derrick's cheek. "You'll be okay, she said to Derrick.
I've been praying hard…and prayers work. They say, bad
boys die before their time…but you got a praying Mama," she
said confidently.

"That's right Mama," Darius agreed. "I'll be back
though, I'm about to take Ericka home."

Ericka stood up, still in a daze not really knowing what
to say. She looked at Derrick one last time hoping he would
recover well.

Darius wanted to give Ericka some time to get herself together, but couldn't help but making hints on the ride home. "Anytime you ready to talk, I'm ready to listen," he said.

"I really don't feel like it Darius. It's so scary…I hate even thinking about it."

"Now, Ericka you have to tell me what happened," he said as he turned the corner onto the busy highway.

For minutes she said nothing. Simply remained in a daze.

"Ericka, I can help. Just tell me," Darius said. He spoke with a lower tone than usual and was careful with his choice of words.

"It happened so fast. I mean there's so much, much more than what happened tonight," she said.

"What do you mean?"

"Well…I mean…I don't know. We went to the movies. And before we came home he stopped at the gas station. Then this boy called him over. They were talking and Derrick tensed up. Then the boy shot him. There was so much blood…so much…" she said as she looked down at her hands.

"Did you know the boy?"

"No…well I guess you could say a little."

"What does that mean?"

"He was at my school, but not as a student. He knew me, and he knew that I knew Derrick."

Darius sat in deep thought for a moment. Just s the light turned red, he turned to show Ericka his crinkled eye-brow.

"So, did you see what he looked like?"

"Yeah, I could never forget his face. And those green eyes."

"Green eyes? Is that what you said?"

"Yeah. Who is he? Why do you and Derrick get so tense when I say that?" she fumed. Now Ericka was getting angry. So much was going on around her but she knew so little about it. She felt like a fool.

"Darrel Simmons. That's his legal name. But we called him Eyes. Not because of his eyes but because he was the lookout. He could see anybody coming from a mile away. Derrick and I used to deal with him under the same boss, who we call Boss. Right after I stopped dealing, Derrick and Eyes were both put on a big project. They were sent to make some big trades with some guys from New York. They were supposed to take most of the money to the Boss but Eyes got greedy, real greedy," Darius explained.

"He took the money?" Ericka asked, wanting to know more.

"Well, he took his cut and Derrick's cut too. Then he disappeared. Derrick didn't know until Boss counted the money. Seeing as though there is a no snitching rule, Derrick took the fall and had to pay out his pocket for the missing money."

"Okay, but I don't understand, if Derrick didn't snitch on Eyes, why is he still after him?"

"Because Boss is mad at Eyes for leaving without a trace. Eyes must think that Derrick snitched about the money. That could've been what they were talking about before he shot Derrick. I don't know, I'll have to wait until Derrick wakes up."

"Oh, if that's the case, somebody needs to tell Eyes so he can chill," Ericka suggested.

"I don't know if it's that easy. We need to find him first. And even if we do, Eyes is stubborn. How are we supposed to get him to listen?"

"I don't know. Just call me if you think of something and please call me when Derrick wakes up."

As Darius was leaving, Ericka's mother was coming in from her night out.

"Wh-what yooooooooou doing here, Derrick?" she slurred. "I- I –I- I thought you got shot up!" she spat.

"No, um, I'm not Derrick," Darius explained as he backed away from her.

"What? You aint Derrick? I'm not that drunk. I know what you look like, fool!" She stumbled to the left, then to the right. Ericka's face instantly became flushed.

"No, Ma, remember? I told you that Derrick has a twin?"

"Oh…Oh yeah. Hold up you dating both of them. Oh Lord now my daughter is a…"

"Ma, no he just brought me home from the hospital," Ericka interrupted.

"Whatever you say. I told you about those boys. Besides, don't you know bad boys die before their time?"

Ericka's mouth hung low. It was the second time she'd heard that weird comment.

"Ma, just…please go to bed. I'll bring you some aspirin upstairs."

"Ummmm…mhhh," she said stumbling her way up the stairs.

"Darius, I'll talk to you later. I have to tuck my mother in," she said escorting him to the door, and closing it behind him.

═══════════════

Ericka woke up the next afternoon around twelve to the sounds of her mother vomiting in the bathroom.

"Ma, are you okay?" Ericka asked, as she held her mother's weave back and rubbed her back.

"Why are you talking so loud? My head hurts," her

mother moaned.

"Hold up, let me get you some extra strength Tylenol," Ericka said.

Unfortunately, when she looked in the medicine cabinet, it was bare. Her mother had used the last of the Tylenol on her last hangover.

"Sorry Ma, it's all gone. I have some of the regular aspirin I gave you last night."

"Naw….naw….naw! Please go to the store and get some with some ginger ale and some of them saltine crackers too."

"Okay, I'll be back in twenty minutes," she said, as she left the bathroom.

"HURRY UP!" her mother moaned.

Erica quickly got dressed and headed out to the store. As Ericka was walking she all of a sudden felt a little paranoid, like someone was watching her. But she put it out her mind as she briskly walked to the store.

Lord please, don't let my mind be playing tricks on me, she thought.

But her mind wasn't. Just as she crossed past an alley way someone grabbed her and covered her mouth to muffle her scream. Her initial thought was that someone was mugging her, but when her eyes met those evil green eyes she knew it was more. Before Ericka could say anything, Eyes pulled a gun in her face.

"Your little boyfriend made it this time but I swear, baby girl, he's not gonna make it next time," he threatened, as his grip tightened on her arm.

"Ow! Look you don't have to…"

"Shut up girl! I've been hearing about the two of you. I hear he tells you everything. How much do you know?"

"What are you talking about?" Ericka asked with fear in her voice.

"You know what I'm talking about! I know he told you something. He runs his mouth like a girl!

"Darrel, wait you don't under-"

Before Ericka could finish her statement, Eyes hit her over her head with the butt of his gun. Ericka was out cold and Eyes walked away like nothing had happened.

━━━━━━━━

Ten minutes later …

"Hey, honey!" A voice called out as a hand reached out and shook Ericka from her from her dazed state of mind.

"Hmmmmmmmm," she moaned.

Ericka opened her eyes, and put her hand on top of her throbbing head. She looked up and saw and old lady standing over her with her cane. She was dressed shabbily but seemed harmless.

"Are you okay, honey?" she asked.

"Yes, Ma'am. I was…"

Ericka was about to say what happened to her but decided against it.

"What happened?"

"I was mugged by a junkie. He took my money, then knocked me out cause I only had food stamps," she lied.

"Are you going to be okay?" the old lady asked.

"Yes, Ma'am, I'm going to be fine," Ericka said, as she brushed herself off and continued her trip to the store.

"I better keep this to myself for now, she thought.

━━━━━━━━

Ericka acted as if nothing happened, when she walked back into the house to take care of her mother. She forced herself to have a half-way decent smile on her face as she emptied the contents of the bag onto the table. Thoughts infiltrated her mind. She thought about calling the police....then Darius...then she decided against them both.

"Ericka where did you get that red mark on your head? It looks like it's turning colors," Ericka's mother said to her while she was fixing her tea.

"Oh, you know the kids are so bad around here. They were throwing stuff out of the window, and something hit me. It was just a little toy though, so it didn't cut me or anything," Ericka said quickly.

"Oh...whose kids? I know May's children are in Florida with their father so..." her mother said, digging a little into her lie.

"On...um...you know I didn't see them real good they were over by Mosher Elementary, so I didn't get a good look at all of them. But trust me, I'm fine, Ma."

"Oh, alright, just be careful next time. Don't even walk that way."

"Gotcha." She nodded.

When Ericka finished with her mother, she decided to call it a night. Besides, the bump on her head was killing her. As she laid in bed she began to think. *How did I get in this mess, and all over a boy. I don't even know how he really feels about me. I should have taken my mother's advice and left him alone. Now look at me, I'm caught up. Lying to my mother, that's not me. He can't even leave them streets alone to be with me. Well, he needs to make a choice and soon, because I'm not gonna let this mess up my future. Drama, drama, drama. I do not need this right now. And to top it all off I think I'm falling in love with him.*

As Ericka drifted off to sleep she said a silent prayer for Derrick.

"Lord, I need your help. Please help me get Derrick out of this. I don't want Derrick to die. Help him change his lifestyle. I want to be with him, but only if he changes his life. Amen."

———————————

Ericka's cell phone rang about five o'clock that next evening.

"Hello."

"Hey, it's Darius."

"Hey, what's up Darius?"

"Nothing much. Derrick woke up. He's asking for you."

"I'm glad he woke up, but I don't know if I can see him right now. Well, I can but…"

"I understand."

"Did you talk to him about Eyes?" she asked.

"No, I might not be able to talk to him until we go home. The police are all over his room asking questions."

"I kind of figured that. Um…I…I saw Eyes," she said hesitantly.

Shocked, Darius' tone deepened. "You did? Where?"

"Yesterday. He pulled me into an alley while I was on my way to the store. He must've been following me." The thought of Eyes made chill bumps pop onto Ericka's arms.

"Did he say anything to you? Did you talk to him?" Darius spoke with speed.

"Well, he told me that Derrick made it this time, but he won't make it next time. He thinks that I know something. He thinks that Derrick is telling me stuff. He said he's heard a lot about the two of us. I think he's been watching me. And then he knocked me out with the butt of his gun."

"A gun! He had a gun in your face? Wow, he on some retaliation type stuff. He almost never uses a gun."

"I can't tell. I've never had a gun in my face before Darius. I've got a bruise on my forehead. I could barely sleep last night. I…I just don't know what to do. I'm so scared right now. I just don't feel safe coming out by myself," Ericka uttered with tears streaming down her face.

"I'm on my way to get you."

Click.

═══════════

At the hospital, police were asking everybody questions.

"Derrick, did you see who shot you?" a plain clothes officer asked.

"No," he answered sharply.

"Derrick, do you know why somebody would shoot you?"

"No."

"Derrick, we'll ask you again."

"Look I don't know anything. I was at the gas station and I got shot- that's it!"

Derrick was very irritable. The pain medicine wasn't really working anymore and every time he made a certain move there was a sharp pain. All Derrick could think about was what could've happened if Ericka wasn't there. He also couldn't thank his brother enough for giving him blood. The police finally left when they figured out that they weren't getting any answers from him or his brother. When Ericka did show up Derrick was ecstatic that she had finally come. Her voice was the last voice he heard before he'd entered unconsciousness, so he wanted to see her badly.

"Hey, baby girl," Derrick uttered.

"Hey, how you feeling?" Ericka asked as she kissed his forehead.

"I'm all good. Better, now that you're here."

Ericka just smiled. It was crazy how just like that Derrick had his wild personality back.

"Where did Ma go?" Darius asked.

"They went to get something to eat," Derrick replied.

"Good, so we're alone," Darius announced.

"Why you say that?" Derrick asked.

"Because we need to talk to you about Eyes."

"Man, I don't want to talk about him. Not in front of Ericka."

"She already knows. Besides, you already got her involved. He's been following her around, Derrick. He hit her over the head with a gun yesterday, so you better start talking. You better say something. What did you say to him before he shot you?" Darius fumed.

"He hit you in the head with a gun, Ericka?" Derrick asked in awe.

"Yeah. He followed me. I think he knows where I live," Ericka said showing him her bruise.

"I'm going to kill him." Derrick fumed.

"No, Derrick you're already in enough trouble. He could've killed you!" Ericka yelled.

"No, he won't. He asked me why I snitched on him. I told him that I didn't. He said he didn't believe me. I told him to call Boss. Then that's when he shot me," Derrick informed.

They were all silent for a minute. They didn't know what to say to each other. Ericka was so afraid, she started to cry. "I can't believe all of this."

"Ericka please stop crying. I hate to see you cry, Yo. C'mon, stop." Derrick begged.

"What do you expect, Derrick? I'm scared. This man knows where I live. He probably watches my every move. I'm terrified, for myself and for you. I bet he's going to try and kill you again. I don't think I can handle that," Ericka admitted. She was fed up, after everything she had been through

"Derrick, come on now, it's time to give up the street life. We did this when we were starving, and Ma couldn't support us. Things have changed- it's time to give it up," Darius said, trying to convert his brother into the right lifestyle.

"No, I need to tie up loose ends first," Derrick said, mainly talking about Eyes.

"No, let Boss take care of it. Here, I'll call him for you," Darius insisted.

"No. I can do it by myself!"

Derrick was just as stubborn as Eyes was, and that was what both Ericka and Darius feared the most. If one of them wouldn't come to their senses then they would both meet their demise.

―――――――――――

By the time Monday rolled around, Ericka knew the day would prove to be grueling. As soon as she made it through the school doors, Tina walked up to her.

"Hey girl. How did you and Derrick's date go?"

"I don't even want to talk about it," Ericka replied.

"That bad, huh?"

"Yep. And I don't know how much more I can take," she sighed.

"Well, girl spill the beans, what's up" Tina asked.

"To start, Derrick took me out on Friday in his mother's car. His license is suspended by the way."

"What…again? Didn't he get in trouble for that last year?"

"Yes, and when we were on our way home he stopped at the gas station. He ran into that boy that has been asking me questions."

"The one with the green eyes?"

"Yep." Ericka tried to continue the soap-opera style story but instantly broke down. "They had words, and then all of a sudden the boy pulled out a gun, and just shot him in the chest."

"Oh no, is he alright?" Tina asked with a concerned look. She reached over and gave Ericka a huge bear hug.

"Yeah, he'll be fine. I'm just worried because the boy attacked me on the way to the store on Saturday and told me to tell Derrick he won't be so lucky next time."

"Ericka, what are you gonna do?" Tina asked

"I don't know. I ain't wit this ride or die lifestyle. Derrick said he would handle it. I just don't' want to see him get hurt again or have something worse happen to him."
Tina grabbed Ericka and hugged her tightly one more time.

"You know I got your back and whenever you need me just call."

"I know girl, Derrick will be discharged in a few days so I will call you so you can come over."

"Alright."

Suddenly, the first period bell rang. Both friends hugged and headed to their classes.

═══════════

Two days passed, and Derrick was home and on the move already. Darius couldn't do anything to stop him. He tried calling Boss, threatened to tell their mother everything that had gone down, and even fought his brother….nothing worked.

Everything seemd to be spiraling down hill. Derrick couldn't find any trace of Eyes. Boss hadn't had any contact with him either. Derrick reluctantly told Boss everything that happened. Boss was proud of Derrick for not snitching, even if it meant getting in trouble with him. Boss said that he was going to try and get to Eyes, and that he was going to help keep an eye on Ericka for him.

"So, you must be feeling better?" Ericka asked, as she opened the front door for Derrick.

He walked inside, and stopped to kiss the side of her cheek. "Everything's fine. I'm feeling much better. I never got the chance to thank you." He grinned.

"You don't need to. But I really wanted to talk to about what you've been doing," she said.

"What have I been doing?" Derrick asked. Guilt had spread all across his face.

"I don't know, but why don't you tell me? I want the truth!" Ericka said with bass in her voice. "Don't tell me it's nothing, cause I can feel it here," Ericka said, pointing to her heart. She made sure to stare Derrick deep into his face.

"Ericka…I…I'm just tying up some loose ends. That's all."

"Derrick, please don't do anything stupid. I really don't want to lose you. I just…I just want you to live a decent life….not always looking over your shoulder," she uttered while fighting back tears.

"I won't… I promise," he said.

All Ericka could do was take his word for it, but inside it was tearing her apart that she couldn't hold on to him. She wanted to do something to stop him from doing whatever it was that he already had on his mind. Ericka already knew that no one could stop him.

═══════════════════

Three weeks passed and nothing out of the ordinary happened. Ericka felt a little safer, and she was less worried about Derrick being hurt. *Maybe Boss had gotten in touch with Eyes, to straighten the beef.* She'd been told that there was no trace of Eyes anywhere. No one had seen or heard from him in weeks.

"Ma, I'm about to go wash clothes, do you need anything washed?" Ericka yelled upstairs.

"Yeah, wash my work outfit, I want to wear it tonight,"

her mother yelled back. Ericka grabbed up the outfit and put the pieces in her dirty clothes bin.

Hmmm...should I wear my Mickey Mouse slippers or my clogs? Well, Derrick bought these so I'll just put these on, Ericka thought to herself.

She grabbed her bag of quarters and made her way to the laundromat around the corner, less than three blocks from her house. As she walked the dark streets, she sang aloud a new tune by Omarion, her favorite artist, called Never Gonna Let you Go, She's a Keepa. It was perfect and fit to a tee what Ericka felt in her heart.

I was as wrong as I could be
To let you get away from me
I'll regret that move for as long as I'm livin
But now that I've come to see the light
All I wanna do is make things right
Just say the word and tell me I'm forgiven

As she sang, thoughts of Derrick invaded her mind. In her heart, she wanted to be with him forever. She figured if she could convince him to apply to Johnson C Smith in Charlotte, North Carolina, they would be able to spend every day together if they both got accepted to the same college.   It would give her a chance to go off to college and not worry about cheating with other boys, and it would surely give Derrick a new start in life.

Just as Ericka neared the front door of the Laundromat, she noticed movement behind a parked car. The Laundromat was packed and well lit, so she keep singing and marched inside. Little did she know, she was being watched. Watched by someone who meant her no good. Without hesitation, Eyes opened up his cell phone as he waited outside the Laundromat and called Derrick's cell.

Derrick answered cheerfully. "What's up?"

146

"What's up snitch?"

"Eyes. Mannnnnnnnn, what you want? I've been looking all over for you. We need to talk," Derrick said firmly.

"Yeah, I heard you've been looking for me."

"Who told you that?"

"Well, you know the street talks."

"Where are you?" Derrick asked.

"Don't worry about that. But you know where you
messed up?" Eyes questioned, disregarding Derrick's question.

"No, why don't you tell me."

"With her. You fell for her. I bet you bought her those
Mickey Mouse slippers, didn't you?" Eyes sneered.

"What?" Derrick said. He immediately remembered
the Mickey Mouse slippers that Ericka had begged him for
some time ago.

"You should tell her that she shouldn't walk outside
with slippers on…it makes it difficult for her to run," Eyes
snickered.

"Eyes I swear if you touch her-"

"Shut up snitch! You cry too much."

"Eyes, leave her out of it…hello?"

Derrick looked at his phone and saw that Eyes had
hung up. He immediately called Ericka's cell phone.

"Hello?" Ericka answered.

"Ericka, where are you!" Derrick yelled through the
phone.

"I'm at the laundromat. Why what's wrong?"

"Stay there, and don't move! I'm on my way okay."

"Okay, but just tell me what's wrong."

"I'll tell you when I get there," he said, then hung up.

Ericka got nervous and scared. She had never heard
Derrick sound so panicky before. Derrick got to Ericka in ten
minutes flat.

"Are you okay?" he asked as he grabbed her arm.

"Yeah I'm fine. What's wrong?"

"What are you doing out this late? And by yourself too? What's wrong with you!" He scanned the entire Laundromat as sweat poured from his face. "Where's Tina? And why didn't she come with you?"

"Derrick! Relax, please your brain is going a hundred miles a minute and your mouth is too. I'm washing clothes like normal people. And I like washing at night, you know that." She placed her hands on her hips. "I don't normally wash with Tina. What's wrong anyway, what happened?" Ericka screamed.

Derrick looked around again, and saw that he had made a fool of himself in front of the few people who were still in the laundromat.

"I'm sorry come on let's just go."

Derrick grabbed Ericka by her arm forgetting that she had clothes to carry home.

"Derrick, help me with this basket. I'll just wash tomorrow. I'm blown," she said, handing him the basket and smacking her lips.

Derrick remained quiet as they headed to the trunk of his car to put the bags inside. Derrick was so deep in thought that he didn't hear Eyes sneak up on them. Although they were in the laundromat parking lot where the area was fairly lit, Derrick's car was positioned in a less traveled area.

"So, I guess she got your ears plugged too, huh?" Eyes said, startling both Derrick and Ericka.

Ericka prayed that someone would look over and see them with Eyes who had a dark hoodie pulled over top of his head.

"What do you want?" Ericka asked boldly.

"I want this snitch dead, that's what I want." Eyes raised his gun at Derrick. Ericka jumped in between the two.

"Darrel, this isn't worth it," she said.

"Ericka what are you doing?" Derrick yelled.

"Why do you keep calling me that like you know me or something? Derrick I thought we was cool, but I guess the money got to your head, huh? Well, I know the feeling I guess it spreads easily." Eyes said, now pointing the gun at Ericka. Ericka's heart raced, but she didn't back down.

"Look, man, I don't know what you talking 'bout. I told you to call Boss!" Derrick said. He tried to keep cool, but still thought about the easiest way to get out of the situation.

"Oh, don't play dumb with me. You thought it was going to be easy huh! Just say the name, keep the money, and move on? No! I told you the streets talk. Why else would Boss be looking for me huh! And why is your gurl talking to me like she knows me? Like she heard so much about me that she knows me?" Eyes said. He was furious.

"Well, I didn't say that I know you but you are much more than Eyes, that's just a street name that made you who you are now. I'm not going to let you shoot him. Please you don't even know what's going on. At least just listen to him," Ericka said as she started to cry.

"Are you willing to die for him?" Eyes asked as he cocked the gun.

"Ericka, move!" Derrick said pulling her toward him.

"No, Derrick you have to talk to him! Make him listen!" Ericka yelled.

Eyes was laughing like crazy. He loved the drama. Suddenly, he pointed the gun at Ericka, because she was directly in front of him. He turned from his right to left making sure nobody was outside the Laundromat, or even watching from inside.

He hated how Ericka had Derrick wrapped around her finger, and hated Derrick for snitching. He'd decided to take away the very thing that meant the most to Derrick.

"**POP**!" Eyes had pulled the trigger.

He stood there for a minute and looked at what he had done. Filled with satisfaction he smiled his evil grin. People inside the Laundromat scrambled to come outside, and some pressed their heads against the window to watch from inside. While there was a scream in search of help, Eyes just strutted away, chest high with pride. Everyone standing around wondered if the person on the ground had died instantly.

═══════════════

Four days later, Ericka entered the hospital with her crew. She knew they all loved her, because they'd given up the opportunity to compete in a dance contest just to remain by Ericka's side.

"Wait down here," she instructed. "Derrick was unresponsive and still on life support when I left last night."

She shot them all a fake-smile. The truth was that Ericka had been crying for days , and nothing but Derrick recovering one hundred percent would make her feel better.

"I think I should go with you," Tina said sassily.

"No, Tina…stay here. Derrick's mom doesn't want a lot of people up there."

"Okay, anything for you. But I'm here if you need me."

"I'll be fine," Ericka said.

"Are you sure?" Tina said, hoping to go with Ericka.

"Yeah, I'm good."

By the time Ericka made it upstairs, Derrick's mother and brother were waiting for her at the door.

"He still hasn't responded, and his vital signs aren't good," Mrs. Windsor said sadly. " They don't think he's going to make it," she added tearfully.

"Can I talk to him?" Ericka asked.

"Sure, maybe he'll respond to you," Darius said.

Ericka slowly made her way to Derrick's bedside. She sat closely beside him and held his hand while the machines sounded off, one after another.

"All I wanted is for you to do better. That's all." Ericka started to cry. "You don't understand how much I love you," she cried. Then she felt his hand squeeze hers. She looked up at him and noticed that he blinked. "He blinked!" she shouted.

Darius and his mother moved closer, but didn't see any sign of blinking. They all continued to watch for a sign of anything. But nothing happened.

"Derrick, you may have a breathing tube down your throat, and can't speak, but I can look in your eyes and tell that you want to talk. It's okay baby," she cried, and rubbed his hand repeatedly with her right hand.

Suddenly, several tears fell from Derrick's eyelids.

"It's okay. Just wait until you get better. I know you hear me." She smiled, then rubbed the side of his cheek with her left hand trying to comfort him.

Derrick squeezed her hand lightly, enough for his mother and brother to recognize that there was some movement.

Ericka smiled. Seconds later, Derrick's eyes closed and the heart monitor went off. His hand loosened from their hand embrace.

"Derrick!" Ericka called out to him. "Derrick!"

The doctors and nurses rushed in, and moved quickly to bring him back. Panic broke out in the room.

Derrick's mother screamed to the top of her lungs, "My son….my son…not my son!"

They tried vigorously, but nothing could be done. They couldn't save him. Ericka couldn't believe it. She simply cried uncontrollably for several long minutes until his mother asked to be alone with her son.

Ericka headed downstairs to tell the girls that Derrick had just passed away. When her friends saw her coming toward them with tears in her eyes, they scrambled to their feet.

"Ericka, what's wrong?" Tina asked as she walked toward her.

"He's gone…Derrick…he just…" Ericka sobbed.

"Oh my God!"

The rest of the girls chimed in as they all embraced Ericka in a mini huddle. All she could do was cry and accept the love.

As days moved forward, Eyes quickly got word that Derrick had died. His satisfaction quickly turned into regret when Boss told him everything. Boss didn't even kill him, because he said that Eyes didn't deserve death. Eyes turned himself in after that. The guilt had gotten to him. Ericka couldn't believe that he was gone, and wasn't used to life without him.

Eventually, though, Ericka got past the grief and depression. She had gotten accepted to both Johnson C Smith and the University of Baltimore, deciding to stay in Baltimore majoring in law.

Derrick still pops in Ericka's head sometimes. Ericka realizes now that she couldn't stop what Derrick was doing, and she couldn't stop Eyes either. Being a part of such a catastrophe only made Ericka realize that sometimes love doesn't conquer all, and she stays far away from people who are addicted to fast money.

But even still, to this day Ericka wonders if Derrick realized that bad boys die before their time.

BACKSTABBER

by Nyomi Simmons

Have you ever wondered who your true friends really are? Sure you have. Each and every day teenagers are faced with friend issues. It's normal from what I've been told. But honestly, my situation nearly killed me because I thought the phrase BFF really meant Best Friend Forever. Sit back and relax while I share my story.

It all started on a Thursday afternoon, two o'clock sharp. The bell rung just as Jayda called out to me.

"Hey Danielle, wait up."

I'd grabbed my stuff off my desk and was headed to the door. I turned to wait even though everyone else had quickly filed out of Mrs. Taylor's seventh grade science class. I hated the fact that Jayda was so slow. She moved as if her one-hundred and forty pound frame weighed her down. Maybe it was her weight. She was the shortest in the class, and quite honestly, the widest. Her hips spread about as if she were an older woman who started out with a cute shape in her younger days. Still in all, she was my girl and the one I called my BFF.

"Girl, come on. Why are you moving so slow!" I shouted. "Stuff those papers in your book bag and let's roll, Jayda."

I stood in the doorway with my hands on my hips waiting for Mrs. Taylor to finally look up. She'd been shuffling through her papers ever since the bell rung. I guess she didn't

care how long it took Jayda as long as her next class hadn't
showed up.

It took a few more minutes, but I'd finally gotten my
girl out the door. I walked faster than she did down the long
crowded hallway. Seventh period, the last period of the day
was next and the teacher didn't play, so I needed to get to my
locker within three minutes flat. Before I knew it Jayda
seemed to lag slightly behind. She started rambling about
some boy in the eighth grade who she had an eye on.

"Is he cute?" I asked stopping in front of my locker.

"No, I like them ugly," she responded sarcastically.
"Of course he's cute," she added while rolling her eyes.

"Well, I just asked. The last boy you told me you liked
ended up getting pimples all over his face."

"You got me on that one, but don't act like you pick
the cute ones…what about Sedrick?"

"What about him?"

"His nose is huge. And his head is running closely behind. Maybe that's why they call him Big Sed."

We both laughed loudly as I checked my lip gloss in
the small mirror. It would've been nice to check my hair since
Sedrick was in my next class, but the sound of the seventh period bell startled me. Instantly, I slammed the door making
the locker shake. Before I knew it, I had jetted down the hall
leaving Jayda in the wind.

"I'll see you after school," I yelled, combing through
my long, thick hair with my hands. "Meet me by the corner
store."

I opened the door to my social studies class and smiled
as soon as I hit the threshold of the door. The class was organ-
ized by three long rows with roughly nine students seated one
behind the other in each row. Sedrick sat in the last row near
the window staring directly at me. His dark skin always
seemed to send chills through me when I saw him. I smiled,

then he smiled back exposing his bright white teeth. Whether he knew it or not, he needed a slot to do a commercial with Colgate. Finally, I refocused on getting to my chair, hoping the onlookers didn't see me blush.

Seventh graders were notorious for starting rumors and I didn't want nothing to pop off so close to Thanksgiving break. I had planned on running for class President and didn't need any boyfriend drama ruining it for me. Clearly, if any of Sedrick's fake-me-out girlfriends got wind of the two of us, they'd hate on me for sure and trash a vote for me.

It always amazed me how popular he had become. He wasn't your normal drop dead gorgeous guy, yet he had charisma. All the girls loved his style. He sorta walked and talked like Jay Z, yet he was three times as dark.

"Psssss," I heard a slight whisper come from behind.

I ignored it and pulled out my composition book. I needed to get my social studies warm-up done before Miss Hill's alarm clock sounded. She was a stickler about warm-up lessons and she was in charge of Student Government which governed the Class offices for all grades. It was important for me to make a good impression while in her class so I copied my work and ignored the constant attempts to get my attention.

"Hey, you hear me," the voice sounded with a higher pitch.

I turned all the way around in my seat with an irritated grimace on my face. "What is it?" I asked Lacie.

She started mouthing words as if I really understood what she was saying. Before she could continue, I waved her off and glanced back over to Sedrick who sat three chairs in front of her. It was crazy, because she wouldn't give up. Within seconds, she started waving a small sized poster in the air that read 'Danielle for President'.

I smiled yet turned around to focus on Miss Hills's

squeaky voice. As she spoke, I wondered what made Lacie become one of my cheerleaders all of a sudden. After all she didn't *really- really- really* dig me like that. Of course she always pretended to be my girl, but I'd heard on numerous occasions that she talked about me behind my back often. I didn't care too much, because she was mostly Jayda's friend, lived in her neighborhood, and they visited each other's home. She'd never been to mine and wasn't gonna get invited anytime soon.

My mother was known to act up when I brought girls home with obvious attitude. Her buzzer would definitely sound off if I allowed Lacie in the house. She was tall, slender, pretty in the face, and reminded me of Rhianna, except for the sassy personality. She called it outgoing, I called it being a loud mouth.

All of a sudden, Miss Hill stopped right in front of my desk. I hoped she hadn't sensed that I was day dreaming.

"Danielle, what do you think about that?" she asked with a firm voice.

"Ahh…I think it's great."

"And…." she said wanting me to elaborate.

I had no idea what she was talking about. I figured if I came clean and told her I wasn't paying attention, it would be better than making a fool of myself. I began to speak, "Well…"

Sedrick interrupted me. "I agree with Danielle," he said out loud. "I think it is great for all countries to work together to solve the problem. If we don't we'll live more undesirable lives."

My face remained flushed. He had given me some idea of what the question was about and saved me all at the same time. I breathed deep inside with a sigh of relief. I knew Miss Hill had fallen for it, because Sedrick was a charmer. What he lacked in looks he made up in charm, and knew how to make all the ladies smile, including me.

For minutes the class discussion continued until it was time to tie all the conversation in with the daily writing assignment. I hated writing but knew it had to be done. Luckily it wasn't due until the following day. I thought about asking Lacie to help me after school, because she'd done a banging job with helping me write my campaign speech. I had asked Jayda to help, but she ditched me for a football game at her cousin's school. *Why was she my best friend I wondered?*

Jayda had the brains but never wanted to help with anything educational. Now if I needed a hanging partner, a shoulder to cry on, or somebody to have my back, she was there, but homework-no!

Before long, class was over and I'd survived another day at Oakville Junior High. It was a decent school, but a lot of changes needed to take place. I really wanted to be voted Class President so I could suggest several options for change. For one, we needed more school fundraisers, more activities, and more after school programs to keep our students from running the streets. I had so many ideas but needed help in incorporating them into my speech.

I turned to Lacie. "Lacie, you wanna hook up after school today. Maybe meet me at the library." I cracked a slight smile knowing that it didn't sound too appealing. "I need a little help with this assignment. Girl, I'm swamped with work, but I know you're good at it."

"What you gonna do for me?" she asked in a serious tone just before breaking out into a laugh. "No seriously... I can't. I got a hair appointment at 3:30. See, that's what happens when you got short hair. You got the good stuff so no worries for you."

She reached out to touch my hair until I jerked back. I didn't believe her little story about a hair appointment but continued the conversation anyway. "Good hair or not, my mother said she isn't paying for any seventh graders in her house to get their hair done. She does it or my cousin does my homemade-do." I started pulling on a few of my tresses with my forefinger and my thumb.

"Well it looks good to me," Sedrick said walking up in front of us both.

When he touched the back of my hair I felt as if I'd melted and floated up to Heaven. I couldn't resist grinning just a bit, but neither could Lacie. She probably was totally unaware how hard she blushed. I watched her fiercely not wanting to remove my stare, but Sedrick kept talking to me.

"Did you hear me?" he asked. "Where you going after school?"

"To the library," I told him. "I got work to do. Besides, it's the only way I can hang out without my mom getting on me."

"Oh yeah."

"Yep." I turned to look at Lacie. "I thought Lacie was gonna go help me with all this work I got. You know how I hate writing. I'm a math girl."

"Well, I'm no good at writing either but maybe we can help each other." He shot me the puppy-dog face.

"Is that a yes?"

"Ummm…if you want," I said softly.

"Bet. We meeting at the library, right?"

Sedrick touched my hand with his darkened skin. As his hand brushed against mine it reminded me how different we were. He was super dark, and I was super light. They say opposites attract, I told myself.

"I'll see you there I said putting my feet into action. I'd almost forgotten Lacie was still standing there until she cleared her throat. I turned to look at her flustered face. "What time?" she asked.

"What time, what?" I returned.

"Are we meeting?"

"I thought you said you had a hair appointment?"

My face showed the confusion while Sedrick brushed past me to leave the classroom. "I'll be there by four," he yelled over his shoulder.

"See you there."

"Yeah, see you there," Lacie said softly."

I rushed toward the door with an attitude. Lacie wasn't fooling me. She had a crush on Sedrick. It was as clear as the sun on a shiny day. I never responded hoping she wouldn't show up. She was one of those people my mother warned me about. She said, "Friends...I gotta tell you a few things about so-called friends. Remember these words," I remembered her saying. "Hang out with as many associates and buddies as you'd like. But only trust those who earn the right to be trusted. Only then do they become true friends."

I nodded my head thinking about my mother's words. She was right...I had to watch my back.

The next day had come and gone, and Jayda and I were gearing up for the Friday night skate party that our school sponsored every year. We laughed like crazy on the phone talking about who couldn't skate, who thought they were cute, and who liked who within our school.

"Girl, is Sedrick coming?" Jayda asked.

"Not sure," I answered nonchalantly.

"Girl, who you think you fooling, Danielle?"

"What?"

"Stop playing yourself," Jayda announced. "Danielle, it's obvious that you like Sedrick a whole lot. And word has it, he likes you too."

I was glad we were on the phone so my girl couldn't

see my face. I'd turned slightly red just thinking about Sedrick. I did like him a lot. I thought maybe it was even love, but my mom told me it was just a crush. She said I would have tons of crushes and boyfriends by the time I was twenty-one.

Jayda interrupted my thoughts.

"I heard you and Sedrick were all cuddled up at the library yesterday."

"We were not!" I shouted. "He sat beside me…that was it."

"Uh huh. You not fooling me."

I sat quietly. She was right and I knew it.

"Did ya'll commit?"

"What do you mean?" I asked.

"What does it sound like I mean? Did ya'll say I do? You know like go together, boyfriend and girlfriend?"

"No. We just worked and talked only a little. We had company."

"Who?"

"Lacie."

"Why was she there?" Danielle questioned. "Never mind. We'll talk about it later. My mom is dropping me off at the school at 7:30. Plus, Lacie needs a ride so we gotta stop and get her too. I'll ask her when I see her why was she all up on you and Sedrick."

"Umph."

"What's that supposed to mean?" Jayda asked me.

"Nothing really. I'm just sick of her, that's all." I frowned and held the receiver away from my ear. "Does she really have to hang with us tonight?"

"Oh, I'm not crazy. There must be some type of problem with y'all. What's the beef? Tell me…I gotta know."

Jayda breathed heavily into the phone. Her actions told me that she wanted to know badly.

"Okay Miss nosey. If you must know…I wasn't too pleased with the way she stayed in Sedrick's face at the library. She claimmmmmmeddddd she was there to help me but it was obvious she was there to smile all up in Sedrick's face.

"So, you jealous?" Jayda blurted out.

"No, I'm not. I just want her to back off."

"You said there was no official commitment. So, technically he's not yours and you're not his."

"Well, Sedrick is showing up tonight just to be with me," I uttered. "So, she better roll with somebody else tonight," I spoke with conviction.

"Alright, you got it. Claim your man," Jayda laughed.

"I gotta go girl, I'll see you at the party."

I hung up as if I could handle Lacie but in reality I wasn't sure how to handle her. She was the frisky type and way too friendly when it came to Sedrick. Besides, it was difficult figuring out how to tell her to back away from Sedrick. Jayda was right. He wasn't officially my boyfriend. Yes, he liked me but we never confirmed that he was my boyfriend or I was his girlfriend. Then it hit me, we would have to make it official at the skate party. *I needed to hear it come from his mouth.*

Six hours later, I found myself rolling around the rink for the twelfth time grooving to the sounds of T.I. featuring Swizz Beatz's hit song, *Swing Ya Rag*. The beat sounded good to my ears and had my adrenaline pumping. I had already sweated out my neon colored t-shirt that read Princess and my size two, Seven of Mankind jeans. My hair was pulled back into a loose ponytail and sweat trickled down from the sides of my forehead.

It was hotter than the hottest summer day but I kept skating, while keeping my eye on the front door to the gym. I checked my watch again just to make sure I wasn't crazy. Sedrick said he was gonna show up by eight. It was already nine o'clock and he'd become a no show. I didn't want to appear depressed or anything, because it seemed like my girls were waiting for me to have a panic attack. All night Jayda kept asking me what was wrong, then Lacie would ask if I was waiting for Sedrick. I ignored them both and kept skating like I was having the best time of my life. I'd found a few other girls from school to skate with even though we really didn't have much to talk about.

Before long the D.J's voice came blasting through the microphone. He wanted us to clear the floor. I told the girl Nancy from my class that I would check her later. I figured I would a least roll over by Jayda who'd been sitting near the vending machines talking on her cell phone. When I reached Jayda she gave me an eye that said don't interrupt. Then she pointed across the room pointing at Lacie who sat near the entrance of the gym. I wasn't interested in Lacie but realized she was talking to Sedrick. My mouth dropped. I was confused. How did he get skates on his feet that quickly? How long had he been in the gym? I asked myself tons of questions in a matter of seconds, but most importantly, why hadn't he looked for me? I was easy to find and he knew I'd been waiting for him.

The next thing I knew, Lacie had Sedrick leaning over her as she whispered something in his ear. Within seconds, he rose, let out a slight chuckle, then smiled. I was livid. I turned to move in their direction when I heard the DJ announced couples only. The room lights dimmed and so did my heart as Lacie grabbed Sedrick's hand and led him to the floor to skate.

Instantly, I stopped in my tracks. I was so embarrassed.

Everyone knew I had my heart set on Sedrick, especially
Lacie. Then the pain increased as the Chris Brown song, *With
You* began to play. The words were perfect for the moment.

I need you boo,
I gotta see you boo
And the heart's all over the world tonight
Said the heart's all over the world tonight
I need you boo
I gotta see you boo
And the heart's all over the world tonight
Said the heart's all over the world tonight

They skated like two love birds on tour with Disney on
Ice. Their steps were in twine with one another and they
laughed as they took each corner with precision. I especially
hated the way Sedrick had one hand glued to the lower part of
her back. I wanted to cry. I wanted to fight. Why were they
doing this to me? Just as the tears welled up in my eyes Jayda
walked up behind me.

"Uncross your arms," she told me.

"Why?" I snapped.

"It makes you look pathetic."

"What?"

I couldn't believe my very best friend would say such
a thing to me. And it seemed as if she liked seeing Sedrick
make a fool of me. I just stared at Jayda but decided to remain
silent. She needed to explain herself and fast.

"Look Danielle, everyone knows Sedrick is popular.
He may be all up on you most of the time, but he flirts a lot.
You gotta accept that."

I studied Jayda like she was crazy. Where was all the
crazy talk coming from? She was my girl and now telling me
to accept Sedrick flirting with the girls, and right in front of
my face.

"I will not!" I shouted and dropped my arms down to

my side. I jetted out onto the skate floor without a partner and caught up to Sedrick and Lacie. "Can I talk to you for a moment?" I asked Sedrick nastily.

Before he could even answer the DJ came on the mic saying, I repeat, this is a couples skate only. If you do not have a skating partner, please get off the floor."

The three of us looked pretty stupid standing in the middle of the floor while everyone else skating around us. So I asked Sedrick again, "Can we talk?"

"I guess," he said looking at me strangely.

We both skated off the floor over to the side behind the bleachers that had been pushed back for the event.

"What's that all about Sedrick?" My hands pointed toward Lacie's smirk.

"What are you talking about?"

"You know exactly what I mean!"

"Danielle, you need to calm down. What you getting so upset for?"

"You told me we were hanging together tonight. Now you out on the floor couple skating with Lacie."

Sedrick chuckled. "Oh girl, that's nothing. We just skating."

"So, you'd rather skate with her than me?" I whined.

"I'm gonna skate with you too, but don't nobody own me Danielle," he said in a more serious tone. "I'm young and don't need to be tied down to one girl."

My neck jerked backwards. It had me completely tripped out that he would openly say he could be with as many girls as he wanted.

"So we not together, right?"

"No we are not," he shot back. "I mean I like you and all but I got my eye on a few girls. We just cool."

Those last words sent my heart traveling down to my shoe. Suddenly I started twitching, looking from side to side, and rubbing the back of my neck. Shocked, seemed to be an understatement. Sedrick was a straight up heart breaker. He'd made me believe I was the one he wanted to be his girl, but now he was treating me like a piece of trash.

"I'll get up with you later Sedrick."

I turned and jetted the other way. Deep down inside, I prayed he would call out my name so that I could turn around. Slowly but surely I slowed my pace and realized he wasn't gonna call me back to apologize. He was serious and I was destroyed. Before I knew it, I'd made it to the bathroom with tears straddling my cheeks. As I walked up to the mirror my reddish eyes showed the sadness. It was my first heart break and the first time I thought I'd experienced love for a boy.

My mother had spoken about her first heartbreak from a boy several times, although it wasn't until the ninth grade for her. She just never explained that I would feel it in the pit of my stomach. Somehow I felt as if I wasn't good enough for Sedrick. He was a basketball star, popular, and had major confidence, while I felt like nothing. Then it hit me, I needed to tell Jayda. She would be able to lift my spirits, pump me up a bit. I knew we'd talk about him like a dog and figure out who I could like just to get back at him.Quickly, I grabbed a piece of paper towel from the dispenser and wet it a little. I dabbed my cheeks and underneath my eyes lightly. I had to pull it together.

By the time I made it out the bathroom and back toward where Jayda sat, I stopped in my tracks. Sedrick was on mission #2, my girl Jayda. He stood over her laughing, whispering in her ear, and pulling her by her left arm. Although Jayda kept resisting his offer, she grinned in his face like the two had been seeing each other.

I wasn't gonna get played by both Lacie and Jayda so I rushed over to where Jayda and Sedrick were showing their affection for one another.

"Jayda, I need to talk to you for a minute."

"Oh, what's up Danielle."

Her cheeks turned a reddish purple.

"I just need to talk. Alone!" I added in a raised tone.

"Go ahead," Sedrick said, stepping back to allow Jayda space. "Your girl is tripping. She think she own me."

Jayda skated away from Sedrick slowly giving me the sign to follow her. I did just that trying to hide my attitude. When she finally stopped, I circled her for a moment trying to get the lump out my throat. Finally, I had the nerve. "So, Sedrick looked like he was feeling you over there, what did he say?"

"Nothing much," Jayda replied unable to look me in the eye.

"Don't lie to me. I saw that for my own eyes!" I shouted.

"You gotta chill Danielle. You can't get upset just because Sedrick talks to someone else. It's just me."

"He likes you Danielle, I can tell."

"And what if he does," she said to me out of the blue.

We both got quiet. My face turned pale. I tried to hold onto the bottom part of my stomach, because I knew I'd be sick soon. My own girl, a back stabber?

I got my feet rolling as fast as I could. I had to go and didn't care if my mom was outside to pick me up or not. I told her eleven o'clock thinking I would stay at the event until it was over. However, my life was going down-hill.

By the time I made it over to the skate rental booth to collect my shoes it seemed like all eyes were on me. It wasn't clear how many people had watched the altercation out on the floor with me, Sedrick, and Lacie or who had seen me and Jayda discussing the Sedrick issue. But it was obvious there was an issue.

I grabbed my coat from the coat-check booth and

rushed out into the cold air. There was nearly an hour to go before my mother would show up so I decided to walk. It was a stupid decision in light of the bad press my neighborhood had been getting lately, yet nothing seemed to matter at that moment except my feelings.

It took almost ten minutes for me to even make it passed the graveyard, still five blocks from my house. It was spooky and dark but I tightened my North Face coat and kept walking. I started thinking about the young girl from my school who was reported missing over a month ago. It had been blasted all over the local news in Richmond, Virginia and most likely nationwide. The more I thought the faster I walked, huffing and puffing all the way until I finally reached my front porch.

When I rang the doorbell, I got nervous knowing that my mother would want to kill me for walking home alone. Instantly, tears welled up in my eyes from thinking about my upcoming punishment. Then my mind switched to thoughts of Sedrick, then Danielle.

The door swung open, my mother's jaw dropped, and I fell into her arms and started sobbing. I cried out, "He doesn't like me, Mommy!"

"What are you talking about, Danielle?"

My mother just held me tightly as we sat by the front door on the brown, welcome mat. She rubbed the back of my head and repeated, "My baby's first heart break."

We rocked back and forth for nearly thirty minutes as she talked to me about love, crushes, and how relationships really worked. She explained that I was too young to have a *real* boyfriend and nothing would come but hurt from a boy at such a young age. She didn't blame Sedrick. She simply said, "Honey, he doesn't know any better." She did however say that Jayda and I needed to talk. She said Jayda needed a crash course on true friendship and that she was willing to give it to her if necessary.

━━━━━━━━━━━━━━━━━━

Days passed and the weekend had come and gone. I had decided to stay cooped up in the house all weekend and had instructed my mom not to accept any phone calls for me. Crazy thing was, nobody even called. It seemed like all of a sudden I was an outcast, and nobody cared about my feelings. My mother tried to talk some sense into me, somehow nothing seemed to work.

The fact that it was Monday morning, twenty minutes away from the first period bell ringing, and I was still in bed shocked me. I had little motivation and certainly wasn't in the mood for learning. I could hear my mother calling my name so I sat up slightly and stretched. My body felt stiff, mostly from not getting out of bed too much in two days, but also from the emotional stress I had put on myself.

Suddenly, my mother burst through the door, "Danielle, get your butt outta that bed!"

"Mom, I'm not feeling too good."

"Danielle, I was a teen once too. I understand what you're feeling."

She sat down on the side of the bed and looked me deeply in the eye like she felt sorry for me. That's all I needed to confirm that I was a failure. Danielle who couldn't keep her boyfriend, I said to myself.

"Look, Thanksgiving is in three more days. All your cousins will be in town and you're gonna have a great time." She smiled then flipped the covers off of me. "So get outta bed, go to school and face Sedrick. Show him you don't care who he likes, dates, or winks at. There are other fish in the sea."

"Oh my God!" I placed my hand on my forehead.

"That is so old school and corny I might add. Mom I will be the laughing stock of the school if I say that. I'd rather ignore him for a few days and just stay in bed. "

Quickly I yanked the covers back toward me and pulled them way over my head. I mumbled beneath the covers, "Mom can you just let me stay home today? It'll give me a chance to regain my dignity. Pleaseeeeeee," I begged. "You don't understand."

Once again my mother tugged at the covers. I fought to hold onto them but was no match for her hefty hands.

"Listen to me and listen good," she warned. "When you start allowing nonsense to keep you from your education that's a problem. Sedrick is simply not worth it."

"It's not just Sedrick."

"What do you mean?"

"I don't really want to face Jayda. I mean I don't know what to say." I shrugged my shoulders and sat up completely in the bed. "I mean it feels so odd being on the outs with my best friend and over a guy."

I guess my mother finally gave in. She rubbed my shoulders and spoke the words I was waiting to hear. "Alright, get some rest, get this out your system, because you are going to school tomorrow. It's a short week, remember? Wednesday is your last day for the week," she added as she left the room.

A sigh of relief filled my body. I needed time to think about how I would handle Jayda when I saw her face-to-face. A part of me wanted to believe that although she enjoyed Sedrick giving her attention the other night, she was truly my friend and wouldn't let his flirtatious spirit come between us. Then a part of me thought our friendship would never recover. After all, she was supposed to be my girl, have my back in good times and bad, and roll with me no matter what. Instead, she was all up in Sedrick's grill and loved every minute of it.

Out of the blue I started crying. Strangely, not because of Sedrick but because of Jayda. I felt lonely and decided to get some sleep. It didn't take long for my tears to dry. Within minutes, I'd allowed my mind to ease a bit and fell off to sleep. Hours later I was awakened by the phone. I figured my mother had called to check on me.

"Hello," I answered in a groggy tone.

"Girl, why didn't you come to school today?"

I had to adjust my hearing. "Who is this?"

"Who you think it is? It's Lacie. I'm just checking on you?"

I started coughing and faking like I had a sore throat. "I got a cold, that's all."

"Oh well I just thought I'd call you."

In my mind I started thinking, *Call me for what? We're not even close like that.*

Then it happened. The words that took me deeper into depression. Lacie hummed then started…"I hate to be the one to tell you, but Jayda and Sedrick been walking around the school all day side by side. I think they go together."

"Fine with me," I shot back.

"Are you serious?" she yelled into the phone.

"Yep."

"Maybe you're just afraid to approach Jayda?" Lacie pressed on.

I hit Lacie with another short answer, "No need." After all she wasn't worth any more words. She was obviously trying to get me agitated and hopeful in starting a bunch of drama between me and Jayda. Besides, I didn't even know if it was true.

"Lacie, I gotta go. My mother is calling me."

"Okay girl, I'll see you tomorrow. Oh, one more thing," she stopped to say.

"What is it?"

"Don't forget speeches are on Wednesday in the gymnasium. I've been putting up your campaign posters all over the seventh grade hallway today."

"Thanks girl," I said unenthused and hung up the phone.

My skin cringed at the thought of Sedrick and Jayda, but I'd already decided not to let it bother me. I hopped up and searched for my speech. It needed some restructuring. It was time I put a little realism in my speech to teach my peers a thing or two.

It didn't take long for my words to flow freely. At one point in my life I had thought of myself as a poor writer, yet it seemed like my true feelings and beliefs now poured onto the page. I wrote about real life experiences that affected our school as a whole, issues that the seventh grade class needed to work on, and mostly about communication and respect for one another.

Before long, the speech was in its final stages and I was feeling back to normal. I decided to take a shower and wash my hair before my mother got home. It was close to two thirty and the sun was shining. A part of me even wanted to take a walk up to the recreation center after my shower. I figured all the kids would show up about three thirty which would give me a little time to fix myself up real cute.

Suddenly the phone rang. This time I was certain it was my mom. "Yes, mother" I said in a cheerful voice.

"This is not your mother," the sassy voice sounded. "This is Jayda."

"Yeah. What's up?"

"Lacie told me you got a beef with me?"

Jayda's voice sounded more unfriendly than I'd ever heard her speak before. We'd been friends forever and I knew when trouble sounded in her tone.

"Listen, Jayda, I'm not up for the he say she say today. What is it that you want?"

"I just want to make it clear. If you want to fight me then let's do it."

"What are you talking about?" I yelled. "I never said that!"

I found myself yelling into the phone and pacing the floor around my room. "Who told you that?"

"Alecia did, a girl in the 8th grade."

"I don't even know her!" I yelled.

"Well, you do know Lacie, and she told somebody that you were pissed and that I was gonna get what was coming to me."

"I never said that!"

"Well, they're all sorts of rumors passing through the school today." Her voice softened a bit but still had a touch of anger. "Somebody even said you didn't come to school today, because you planned on being outside when the bell rang with your older cousins. I guess to fight me," she added.

"Jayda, why would I want to fight you?" I questioned with attitude.

"I figured maybe because Sedrick asked me to be his girlfriend."

A lump formed in my throat. Then there was silence. Complete silence. More silence.

"You didn't say yes, did you?"

More silence.

Look Danielle, I gotta be honest. You and Sedrick never made a commitment to one another so why should I say no? He likes me and I like him. It takes two. Sorry babe, you liked him but he wasn't digging you," she ended.

One, two, three, four, five I counted inside trying to hold myself back. "You sure are a great friend," I told her.

"I hope this doesn't affect our friendship," she uttered.

"No, not at all. I gotta go Jayda. I'll catch up with you later."

I slammed the phone down and headed to the shower. Jayda was erased from my mind forever I told myself.

The next two days seemed to speed by. It was already Wednesday and time for me to get up in front of the enormous crowd. I stood in front of the podium with confidence as I recited my speech on why I should be the class President of the seventh grade class. I spoke about integrity, loyalty, and all the characteristics that make each and every one of us great. I even touched on progress and how we needed to move forward as a class keeping the negativity out of our school.

I managed to keep a straight face and hold my head up high even though there had been whispers ands facial expressions all day relating to the Jayda, Sedrick and Danielle drama. I kept myself out of it all, never commenting or adding to the drama. Jayda and I had even passed each other in the hallway a few times where she snubbed me and rolled her eyes. I ignored it, and kept focused on my character, the person my mother had raised me to be. I knew Jayda was a better person than that, but unfortunately she'd allowed peer pressure and rumors to mess her up.

As my speech came to a close, I noticed Jayda in the audience. She was sitting alone with reddish eyes as if my speech had caused her to cry. I ended with my last line…Be all that you can be and not what others want you to be. The class cheered like crazy and stood up chanting my name. Hopefully, that was a sign that they would leave the gym and vote for me on the ballots awaiting them in their classes.

As I walked toward the exit of the gym, Jayda called out to me. When I turned the first thing I asked was, "Wow was the speech that powerful that it made you cry?"

"No," she responded, then cracked half of a smile. "Sedrick did."

I said nothing. It could've been a trick.

"He dumped me, Danielle," she admitted. "I guess I deserved it. I knew he was a player and when he switched up on you to give me a little attention I fell for it."

We both started walking out the door considering the principal was shuffling everyone back to their classes. As we walked she explained how she'd made a mistake, especially by listening to all the rumors. By the time I reached my class, I'd verbally forgiven her. I just wasn't sure how much my heart could really forgive her. Jayda didn't realize that she had violated my trust and that had to be earned again.

When I walked into my seventh period class I frowned. It was the worst class of the day, Social Studies, the class I shared with both Lacie and Sedrick. They were both sneaky conniving, and always wore plastic smiles. I brushed past them both and sat down to mark my ballot. I watched as each student got up to cast their vote in the box on Ms. Hill's desk. Sedrick had the nerve to kiss at his ballot then at me before putting it into the box.

I shot him a fake grin and opened my textbook. I started doing my assignment and paid no attention to anyone else. Ms. Hill had instructed us to finish all pages written on the board and not to leave our seats while she conferred with her colleagues and counted the votes.

Before long, she entered the class and sat at her desk. Within minutes an announcement came on over the loudspeaker. As the principal read off the names of the winners for each grade level my heart pounded. When he said Danielle Chiles, class President for seventh grade, my classmates went wild. Although they started jumping up and down, I never left my seat. It seemed like I'd been through a rough two weeks but it was all worth it. A lot of lessons were learned and I would have plenty of stories to share with my cousins over Thanksgiving dinner.

Suddenly, the last bell of the day rung. I hopped up ready to exit when Lacie walked over to me with a big smile.

"We won!" she shouted. "You wanna hit the library today or just hang out a bit?"

I smiled widely. "I don't think so. Maybe you should ask Sedrick," I said, just before walking out of the room.

COMING SOON!!!

Teenage Bluez 4

CALL FOR
STORY SUBMISSIONS

We're now accepting all ideas/submissions for short stories to be included in Teenage Bluez 4. All submissions must be at least 20 pages, but no longer than 30 pages. Stories submitted must not contain any profanity or explicit sex scenes. Male teenage authors are strongly encouraged. All submissions must deal with today's teenage issues, such as, but not limited to: Peer Pressure, Drugs, Sports, or Parents/Teen relationships.

Please submit all stories to submissions@lifechanging-books.net or mail them to:

Life Changing Books

P.O. Box 423

Brandywine, MD 2013

DATE DUE

FOLLETT

Ma   yable to:

(Pers   nd cash)
Mail

Purcha

Name

Addre

City _

State a

Number of books   _____

Shipping Charges (add $4.25 for 1-4 books) _____

Total for this order   _____